"DORINDA TILBURY, DESPITE YOUR VERY FIERY TEMPER, I find you a most attractive and beguiling woman whom I would be honored to know far better," Lionel said.

If fire was not at hand, the soft tone of his words lent force enough to melt that heart of ice which was usually warm and devoted to others.

"May we begin again, Dorinda?" he asked.

"Yes," she said in the lowest of voices.

"Then let me seal it with this," he said, drawing her into his arms and kissing her lips tenderly.

In that one instant, Dorinda thought her whole self aflame. She had never met a man like Lionel Ridgely, so bold and daring, so handsome and passionate. And she tried desperately to fight falling under his spell, but now she thought that impossible. . .

Your Warner Library of Regency Romance

The Pink Phaeton

JULIANA DAVISON

WARNER BOOKS

A Warner Communications Company

For Elizabeth Bromley Rogers
no more blue sitting rooms

1

"Master Cracker, you'd be advised to take that . . . that vehicle back 'round to the carriage house before his lordship sees it. I can't imagine what you was thinkin' of to craft such a . . ." Peg Garetty was visibly unnerved by the appearance of a brightly colored carriage in front of the earl of Balmoral's London townhouse, and for all the world to see!

The stout, kind-hearted servant feared more for the carriagemaker's neck than her own; nevertheless, it was her responsibility to maintain the proper degree of London respectability both inside and outside the domicile.

"My dear Mrs. Garetty, on my life I don't know why you fret so. Just have a look-see," the somewhat spindly gentleman said, wiping a few unruly gray strands of hair across his balding head as he drew a badly crumpled letter from his vest pocket. "Spectacles?" He offered his own.

"It is not my eyes that deceive," Peg quickly answered, not a little insulted. "See here, Master Cracker, the specifications of his lordship are stated in our own tongue." She pointed to the critical words on the parchment.

"That is my point exactly," he said and read the letter aloud. " 'Master Henry Cracker' etcetera, etcetera my own surprise—how terrible and how wonderful! But to appease you, after a short ride, I shall let Master Cracker hide it and Papa will be none the wiser. 'Tis just past ten and he shan't return for luncheon till past noon. Oh, Peg, it is the best gift in all the world!"

"But, Miss, I fear you have—" Peg tried to uncloud the truth, but her efforts were all for nought.

No sooner did the young master and future earl, George Tilbury, a mere lad of eight, appear on the scene than Dorinda spirited him down the steps of the townhouse into the awaiting phaeton after having been assured that his morning studies were completed.

"But what about my horses, Miss Tilbury?" Master Cracker cried out.

"Fear not, Master Cracker, you shall have them back within the hour," she promised as they trotted down Park Lane toward the first gate leading into Hyde Park.

Satisfied with the lady's word, Master Cracker smacked his lips, clapped his hands once and said, "Your worries appear to have been unnecessary, Mrs. Garetty."

It took all of Peg's restraint to keep from boxing the man's ears. "His lordship had no intention of presenting his daughter with a phaeton of her own! This was to serve in the place of the one lost in the Brighton countryside two months past—on the occasion of his visit to the Regent's pavillion," she said in a weighty tone, as though she herself had been there. "Now what am I to tell the earl? And pray who shall tell that sweet young thing that the pink phaeton was a surprise to all? Will you break her heart, Master Cracker?"

Dorinda turned the carriage into the park at Grosvenor Gate and gave the horses free rein on the East carriage path, much to the startled dismay of those wishing to enjoy their own leisurely pace of three miles an

Road, he asked the most rattling question. "Is that the house they say Mrs. Fitzherbert kept while in London?"

"What do you know about it?" The Regent's past amour with the lovely widow was well known; some, in fact, admitted that they now preferred her to the future queen, a Saxon princess. But clearly this was no subject of concern for her brother, named at birth in honor of the Regent's ailing father.

"My friend Master Leroy and I discussed it at great length when we unearthed a copy of the *Evening Herald* and discovered the story. Did you know about *her,* then?"

"George, Papa will have you drawn and quartered if he hears this talk. You'd be a far healthier child, with better prospects of one day coming into your inheritance, if you never mention such things. Now hush and try to enjoy the ride. We've already arrived at the South path," Dorinda said, but she herself could not dismiss the topic so easily from her mind.

She thought of the future king and of the tragedies he had had to face—the loss of his most favored lady love, whom his father would not recognize; marriage to a woman he clearly did not love; and the cruelest blow, the recent loss of his only heir, Princess Caroline and the child she had just borne. Out of a loveless marriage came more sadness, Dorinda thought to herself. *I shall not make such a mistake,* she vowed silently. She counted her blessings for not being born the child of the greatest monarch in the world.

When the phaeton turned off Park Lane onto the walk leading back to their own carriage house, Dorinda saw that Peg and Master Cracker were still enjoying their heated debate. They did not see her unhitch the horses and stow the prized wheelabout in a stall. But when she called to George to fetch a bucket of water for the animals, Peg turned around and saw her mistress, her

down at the mahogany dressing table in the boudoir they shared. She lifted the top of the vanity and Dorinda caught sight of herself in the revealed mirror.

"Well, Sister, I must own up to it. I appear a fright," Dorie said, more amused than ashamed at her dishevelment. She thought it absurd that a woman should always have to look as though she had just stepped from a picture portrait. But she said none of this to Edwina, for fear of further ruffling the dear heart's feathers.

She let Edwina coif her hair, brushing back the blond tresses into a neat chignon. With a tortoise comb that had once been their mother's, Edwina loosened a few curls from the tight bun to fall gracefully at the nape of her sister's neck.

"You've just enough time to change before papa comes home for luncheon. And if you like," Edwina said as she opened her side of the double armoire, "you can choose from one of my new gowns."

"Winnie," Dorinda said, calling her sister by her favorite pet name, "they're beautiful. From what creator did you purchase them?" she asked as she caressed the delicate fabrics—silk, voile, mousseline, velvet, soft cotton lisle. "It's been far too long since I have thought to spruce up my wardrobe."

"But the Ascot season begins only two months hence, Dorie. Surely you must see to your new frocks by then . . . I have it! I shall take you to Beauchamp Place where I discovered a most luxurious shop during my last outing. But until then, you must content yourself with this," she said as she drew from the cupboard a delicate pink velvet afternoon tea dress. "I must confess I was saving it for your upcoming birthday, but it will look terribly smart when you're riding in your new phaeton— that is if papa lets you keep it."

That same questioning look was again on Dorie's face. "Why would papa have commissioned the carriage if he did not intend for me to keep it?"

festivities, Dorie knew of the excitement, the parties, and the dances that were to be. She had thought of the future, of marriage, of sharing the company of the right sort of gentleman: to be courted, to be waltzed across the dance floor, to walk arm-in-arm through the park. But alas, the realities were never quite as wonderful as her dreams. The bubble burst right after the come-out. The gentlemen she met were immature—neither dashing nor witty, however handsome. Not a one chanced to strike her fancy.

In the past three years, she had come to appreciate more and more the life she led in the bosom of her family. Helping her young brother, who was only three when their mother died, to make his way in the world; and being closest companion and confidante to her sister Edwina, these were her greatest concerns and offered far more enjoyable company than any of those who came calling. Yes, she would have liked to tell Edwina not to set her sights too high, but she couldn't dash this happiness Winnie felt, not when it would cruelly dissipate on its own and all too soon.

She thanked her sister heartily for the beautiful gown and, after looking once more in the dressing table mirror that, too, had once been their mother's, she was satisfied with her appearance. They descended to the drawing room, to wait for their papa, the earl of Balmoral.

Much to their surprise, they found him already seated upon the red damask sofa, his pipe and tobacco pouch familiarly posed on the marble sofa table, conversing animatedly with George. George was recounting his earlier excursion through Hyde Park while his father wore a mixed expresson of pleasure and pain on his face. Dorie and her sister exchanged knowing looks and entered the drawing room, all smiles.

"Oh, Papa!" Dorie exclaimed as she walked toward him with open arms. "Dear Papa," she said with a heavy sigh.

daughter to relinquish a life of her own in order to take care of his family.

"Dorinda, I think you know the meaning behind my words. It has been three years since your come-out and not one suitor has caught your fancy, or come up to scratch. And it is certainly no fault of my own. I have sought on countless occasions to introduce you in the right circles, and have paraded such a troupe of young eligibles through this house that one would think it a place for wayward young men, were they not each of fine distinction. But not even one have you liked. And to think that your twenty-first birthday is in only a few weeks. . . . This is certainly not the example I would wish you to set for your young sister who, in only a matter of months, will be joining you in the rank of 'Woman.'

"I must say that I cannot permit you to possess your own phaeton, which will absent you from this house with even more perplexing regularity. In fact, the lack of a roustabout of your own is probably the only thing that keeps you from spending more time with your favored horses. I fear each day you ride in Hyde Park that we will lose you to some highwayman, or some wild boar that still lurks in His Majesty's former reserve," the gentleman said, giving some clue as to his preponderence of white hair.

"Father, you know very well that no such beast has existed in the park since the days of King Henry VIII. In the future, dear Bucky will be at the reins and either my devoted sister, or brother who did accompany me this day, will be at my side. I see no reason why I may not enjoy riding our very own horses," Dorinda said, but began to abandon all hope.

"Father," Edwina interceded, hoping to favorably press home her sister's cause, "I think it terribly unfair for my sister and me not to have a phaeton between us. It is quite the thing to see the other young ladies in Mayfair on riding expeditions about town. I fear people will think

2

"Dorinda, sometimes I think that you have positively lost your senses!"

"Perhaps . . . but I have gained a phaeton."

"And soon after a husband you do not even know!" Edwina retorted.

"One would think *you* the blushing bride to be, what with all your worry," Dorinda said with amusement.

"In truth, my dear sister," Edwina said as she smoothed away the wrinkles that had formed in her lap, "I fear I shall be next on papa's agenda."

"Then you shall follow the example I will set when I propose to talk my way out of it," Dorie suggested with the smile of keen invention on her lips.

"But you heard papa's tone . . . and once he has set his mind on something, there's no relenting," Edwina warned.

"Yes, *his* mind perhaps. But he cannot undertake to make up the mind of my suitor and I think I shall fare better on that account. For, after all, do you know of a man so pressed on becoming a husband that he would marry a woman who cared not a whit for him?" Dorinda asked, pleased with her own logic.

"Papa can contrive to make your dowry quite handsome. Any gadabout with numerous accounts payable to our town's various gaming dens would pounce on an

Until that terrible day when the pneumonia consumed Eloise Tilbury, in Dorinda's sixteenth year, she and her sister had had a pleasant accord, but were not what one would call devoted. Then, the four years that stood between the two girls had seemed an eternity. Edwina was far behind Dorinda in her studies, her appreciation of music, of art, of all the finer things life has to offer. Dorinda was interested in the world outside of London; Edwina's world was that of her dolls and playthings. The distance between them was expected and accepted. George's crying was a constant reminder that there was a baby in the house, but no one save his mother and his nurse Peg had been terribly concerned with anything having to do with him.

Then their world changed and Dorinda was suddenly the lady of the house, ready to assume all the responsibilities of her mama. She had been an eager student of Eloise's when it came to setting the table, composing the menu for a grand dinner, or selecting the music for the pianist—even the less exciting chores that kept their household's momentum.

Dorinda and Edwina each discovered the merits of having a sister to fill the void that now existed in their home. Their papa was unreachable, as he withdrew into his private world—his men's club, his duties at Parliament, even the discreet, occasional visits to a select gaming club, which Dorie accidentally discovered when she started tending to her mother's ledger. Without realizing it, both young ladies turned to Peg, the nurse whose ministrations they had once been so glad to renounce when each had turned eight. Her understanding, her sympathetic shoulder, her needed approval—they knew these were things they would never outgrow. They came to rely on her, as did young George.

When most young ladies would shun the presence of a boisterous little brother, these two welcomed the child in their arms. He was forever at their side, looking about bareback through the fields around their estate, known as Balmoral Court. George would pretend to be her very own groom after watching Bucky, and those who came before that fifteen-year-old lad, as they tended to the horses, curried and groomed them, and even applied special dressings to their hooves and muzzles. It was an eternally idyllic summer, and Dorie wondered what species of husband could be found who would let her continue in what she knew to be questionable pastimes for a young lady of title.

These country recollections filled Dorinda's mind and crowded out the bargain she had made with her father as she took her phaeton once again over the Serpentine bridge in Hyde Park. Ascot was, as her sister had said earlier, only two months away, and she anticipated the opening of their house as never before.

To please Winnie, and herself more than a little, Dorinda spent the next few weeks at various houses of fashion in the hopes of bringing her wardrobe up to par. The sisters were fitted with the smartest new clothes, a different costume necessary for each of the varied social events of Ascot. "The Gentleman's Lady" was every bit as scrumptious as Winnie had described. She recognized Lady Molton, the Countess Derringo and even her highness, Lady DeWitt, adjourning to the various design rooms of the establishment. Edwina was *au courant* concerning the most adept dressmakers in town; nor did she disappoint her sister in her choice of milliners.

At "The Feather in Your Cap Shop," the most fanciful bonnets were created. Dorinda's favorite selection was a wide-brimmed saucer-shaped hat held in place with a great length of voile tied across the crown, under the chin, and artfully wrapped around the neck so that the trail hung bride-like down the wearer's back. Edwina, always the peacock, chose upward of half a dozen, each fashioned with plumes of various colors.

"George will laugh heartily when he sees these,"

she considered to be her first-born as well, crossing herself visibly.

"Oh, dear Peg, have you gone and made a to-do on my account?"

"Never you mind," the widow said, after being satisfied that Dorinda would hark unto her command.

Not long after Dorinda had slipped her slender frame into a silken gown the color of saffron, her sister's head popped, jack-rabbit, into the boudoir.

"*Maquillage?*"

"What did you say?" Dorinda asked.

"*Maquillage*, as the French say. Powders, essences, pomades," Edwina explained, her head full of the images of the Empress Eugenie, whose life most intrigued the young, impressionable English maiden. "If the truth be told, Dorie my love, it would not hurt to accent your beauty in certain strategic spots," she added, sounding more like the Emperor Bonaparte himself.

"Oh, heavens!" Dorinda cried, but nevertheless sat still for the application of kohl to rim her eyes and intensify their emerald quality, of a lustrous pomade which gave her lips the succulence of ripe cherries, of a discreet blushing rouge in a soft yet persistent shade of berry-red to further heighten her high cheekbones.

"Perhaps I should have been the painter of the family," Winnie said, marveling at her work.

" 'Tis far easier to work on a breathing canvas which brings life to itself. Besides," Dorinda said lovingly, "I shall be happy to see you at the pianoforte tonight. As it is my birthday, I shall see fit to give you a summary of my requests."

Edwina heartily accepted the challenge, but as they descended to the drawing room, she could not help but laugh.

"It was not that amusing a request," Dorinda said, in confusion. "I do not understand your good humor."

"Well," Winnie began in a tone that implied a forth-

"Papa, you know that my inheritance will see to all my needs . . ."

"Money alone cannot look out for you. You need a loving husband who will make you the champion of his existence, who will see to it that your every need and happiness is fulfilled," he said, his eyes focused on her, though it appeared he saw not her face, but that of one all too similar—his lost wife.

"I fear that I shall be put out before the week is up," Dorinda said. "Yea, that indeed you have already found a husband for me."

Dorinda looked languidly around the room. Was he there among them, a man she would be forced to share her life with? Which of the colorless bores—boors!—was he?

"Dorinda, all that I ask is for you to prepare to assume the duties of a wife," her father told her, "or to relinquish your coveted pink carriage."

The gaiety of the evening was lost to her now. She confessed, if only to herself, that she had accepted the earl's challenge too hastily, had not fully measured the severity of his words. He did indeed mean to have her married and established in a house of her own—or force her to curtail her favored pursuits. Could she part with her phaeton, should she choose to remain unwed?

Despite all her show of lightheartedness to her sister, her brother, her guests, she could not hide from herself the secret terror she felt at the thought of beginning the kind of life her father wished her to embrace. Perhaps if she could find a man who would love her as deeply as her father had loved her mama, it would not be so terrible. . . . Yet Dorinda could not imagine the man whose love would make her want to leave so cherished a home as hers.

though it was badly marred, with a front wheel broken, it could surely hold her until he could summon a hackney. But as he took her arm, she drew back sharply.

"There's not a thing wrong with me, Bucky. But look at my phaeton. Look what the imbecile has done to my phaeton! Papa will be furious. And there's no means of having the repairs accomplished without telling him. Look at it! That lovely pink hue has been scraped off the sides, the canvas hood savagely slit in two when that horrid, horrid fool attempted to whip his horses back to their senses," she said, and then covered her eyes. "I cannot bear to look at it."

"But then you're wholly well, Miss Tilbury?" he asked. "No damage sustained to your person?"

"Of course I'm all right. But what shall we do about this . . . this mess?"

Bucky was so deliriously relieved that he could not give her a coherent answer on that issue. In his concern for his mistress he had not thought past tending to her needs. Now he tried to turn his thoughts to mending the panorama of destruction that had resulted from their encounter with the forest green coach-and-four, disabled farther down the lane.

"How are we to make amends for the handiwork of that indignant roadhog, that imbecilic oaf, that boorish—"

"Madam . . ." Bucky tried to stop her cascading fury.

"—groom, that savage servant in an unknowing master's employ, that careless—"

"Your ladyship . . ." Bucky tried once again to get her attention.

"Oh, but dear Bucky, I haven't asked after your health. Are you well?"

Bucky merely tilted his head to one side, indicating that they were not alone. Dorinda turned around and saw the tall, handsome gentleman who, by the grin on his

29

the fate of having to answer this impertinent personage, felt compelled to tell the troublemaker who it was he was addressing so familiarly.

"My good sir, I must say that you are speaking to Miss Tilbury. You shall be forewarned that her father is at Parliament this very moment and shall not sit well when he hears of this affair," the groom pronounced imperiously, or so he thought.

"I fear you are mistaken," the gentleman retorted boldly, "for I have yet to hear a lady of title use such profane oaths as this one did when I first approached. A lady finds it in her heart to be forgiving and courteous in even the most unpleasant circumstances."

As he spoke, Dorinda watched him closely. She was entranced by those almost haunting eyes, the wavy black hair, his strong jaw, his terribly, terribly agreeable physique. But a woman's scorn is far greater, at such moments, than any physical attraction. All she could think of was that thing so precious to her had been nearly destroyed by him. Alas, there was no forgiveness in her heart, or her voice.

"You have not yet offered to make the needed amends on my damaged carriage," Dorinda said. "It was your fault. I insist upon satisfaction. My groom will tell you to whom you may make these restorations."

"Restore it to its former state? Damages *I* have caused?" he echoed in disbelief. "It was your groom and not I who caused our mishap."

"*My* groom? You mean to imply that my groom, who has faithfully served my family for three years following his apprenticeship, my groom," she repeated (and here Bucky smiled proudly at his mistress's words of defense), "who has been conducting this phaeton throughout London since it was delivered, *my* groom damaged my phaeton?"

"Your groom was not watching the road," he said firmly. "His eyes were not upon your horses, nor mine,

4

The earl of Balmoral was sitting in his favorite library chair at the St. Regis Club, unaware of what was transpiring on the other side of the city. He was appreciating the warmth of the fire (for, it must be told, his circulation was not what it once had been, the earl coming dangerously close to the age of sixty), when he saw a very dear and old acquaintance enter the room. He signaled to the nearest gentleman's gentleman, and requested that the white-gloved servant ask the marquess of Beaumont to join him for a snifter of brandy. Though the earl had readily recognized the marquess, he did not remember him looking so very much his age. Time had etched its lines deeply on the man's face.

"So good to see you," was the marquess's greeting. "Now let me think how long it has been . . . Three years? Yes, three years. It was at your daughter's come-out if memory serves me. How are you, good friend?"

"In the best of health—barring the occasional arthritic seizures," he said in a mocking tone. "And how is the lovely marchioness? Enjoying the rare country life in Tunbridge Wells?"

"My dear wife fares far better in the country where she can take the waters. Yes, these past years have been delightfully tranquil, not at all taxing as is life in these hallowed walls, as I'm sure you well know. It does my

earl asked, while he pondered how he could best be of help.

"If one dare call it that—my son has not quite kept it up to snuff, not being the host his father once was. We are at the mercy of restaurateurs each evening and a very uncivil maid during the day, my wife's trusted servants having followed us to the country. I must admit that our neglect of Lionel is partly to blame for the present situation . . ." the marquess mused.

"Then I will expect you and your son to grace our table this very evening," the earl offered, as a plot hatched in his mind. "You remember our devoted Mrs. Garetty—she will be delighted at the thought of guests at our dinner table, for I fear that our house is as solemn as yours must be . . ." and here the earl's voice trailed off.

"Then you have not remarried, dear Edmund," the marquess assumed correctly. "No London dowager nor widow has captured your fancy?"

"It has been my main purpose to raise my children, rather than have to cater to the whims of a new wife and, if the truth be said, I doubt I could find a woman comparable to my beloved Eloise. But enough of such talk. We must think of the young. My darling Dorinda will be delighted to see Lionel again. He was taking his studies abroad—was he not?—the last time you visited my home," the earl remembered.

"Yes, indeed. Dorinda and Lionel have not seen each other since they were old enough to play together as boy and girl. That was some time ago . . . And what about your other children?" the marquess asked with great concern.

The earl described in a lengthy summary—as one would expect from a doting, loving father—the events of the past three years. The maturing of his daughters, of his son, his hopes for their futures.

"Shall I have Cook botch the meal?"

"No, no," Dorinda said. "Just because of my ill mood, I shall not have your good name and reputation tarnished. You would do best to follow my father's instructions, and if it would help you excel at the task, I will aid you in the selection of the menu," she offered.

From a high pantry shelf, Peg retrieved a worn leather-bound book.

"This contains some of your mama's finest and best-received dinner menus. I think it only proper that you choose from among these. Lady Tilbury—may she rest in peace—had an uncanny knack for combining tastes that she called 'exotic and familiar' so that, as she told it, there was always something for the food fancier and for the 'artless eater' as well," Peg explained, hoping to give the girl a special sense of her mother.

They perused the tome together. As Peg remembered the particulars of one evening or another, she would share the stories with Dorinda and watch the girl's face light up with joy as she heard more and more about her mother's fêtes. They considered each menu, making notes and adding new suggestions all along. They marked those most suitable and, in the end, chose two, this to ensure Cook a second choice should she be unable to fulfill the first.

Dorinda was about to help Mrs. Garetty shine the silver when she heard a timid knocking at the kitchen door. She stepped forward to answer it but Peg stopped her path, reminding her that the mistress opens only the front door of her home, and only on rare occasions at that. But so constant a knocking had already aroused Dorie's curiosity so that when Peg reached the door, Dorinda was peering over her shoulder. They both recognized the bespectacled young man who stood, shaking, on the threshold.

"Master Turner, you're as white as a ghost and

Dorinda pleaded softly. If it weren't so fearful a situation, she would have laughed at his inadequacies.

"Your brother was thrown from the horse before it quit the palace gardens," he answered matter-of-factly, sure he had already recounted that part.

"Thrown from the horse?" Dorinda repeated desperately. "But how has he been injured?"

"Dear Lord, help this man if he does not speak faster," Peg muttered.

"He is presently in Harley Street," Turner said, in a more pained voice. "He is being looked after by one of the royal physicians himself."

"Peg, we must leave at once," Dorinda said quickly. "Where is your coach, Master Turner?"

"My coach?" he asked, not comprehending.

"Yes, you see our groom is not here presently and no coach is at our disposal. Now where is your coach, so that we may return with you to Harley Street?" Dorinda asked hurriedly.

"But I have none, Miss," he answered in his meek tone.

"Then how did you get here?" Dorinda asked, losing all patience, and rightly so.

"I ran—with all God's speed, straight from that street," he said.

"Good Lord, we are ruined," Mrs. Garetty said under her breath.

"No, Peg, listen. You go out to the lane and call us a hackney coach. I will tell Cook to answer all callers and give word to Winnie when she returns," Dorinda said, thinking quickly for all of them.

"Yes, Miss," Peg agreed, willing to do whatever was required of her.

When Dorinda joined her, there was no hack waiting, only her very impatient sister Edwina.

"Not a hack in sight, Miss," Peg said, wringing her hands.

"I would like to see my brother, if that is possible," Dorinda asked politely. "He must be frightened at these unfamiliar surroundings."

"Usually I'm not allowed to give such permission, but as he is a juvenile, I don't see how it can hurt," the kindly woman admitted.

Dorinda's heart throbbed noticeably within her chest as she walked down the corridor to the room where her brother rested.

He lay motionless on the white cot in the rear of the tiny room. His eyes were closed, his head nestled deep into the pillow. But when George heard footsteps on the floor, he opened his eyes and smiled faintly.

"Dorie . . ." he began in a weak voice.

"Don't try to talk, darling George. It's far more important that you rest," she said softly, brushing his hair off his forehead. But he continued. "I made a dreadful mess . . . and perhaps will cause father to be in a more dreadful muddle with His Majesty."

"A few flower beds overturned will not see papa ousted from Parliament," she said reassuringly.

"My hand . . ." he said, trying to lift it from beneath the thin white blanket that covered his body to his neck. "I remember trying to break the fall, but my arm was not strong enough . . . it gave way. I still feel some of the soreness, though the pain has lessened."

His small hand was wrapped in gauze. Dorinda wondered if his improved feeling was due to not so severe an injury as she had feared, or merely the administration of a powerful drug. Her mind filled with questions as they waited for the doctor. When he appeared in the doorway, Peg, Edwina, and even the ever-shaking Master Turner were behind him.

"How is our young patient?" the doctor asked, with a jovial smile. "Reassured, now that his family has come to claim him? I must say that when his . . . friend," the doctor said, looking at Master Turner, "aided me in

released," he confessed, growing not a little red in the face.

"Oh, dear," Dorinda sighed, realizing that the day's troubles had not yet come to an end. She sincerely hoped that Bucky had returned from solving the first mishap, so that he might aid Master Turner in this other task. "Do you consider the horse deranged?" she asked, dreading the thought of having to put one of the great animals to sleep.

"I have no light to shed on that matter. It was incomprehensible to me why it suddenly behooved the horse to leave the path," he said, regretting the pun as soon as the words escaped his mouth.

Knowing her brother's impatience, Dorinda wondered whether he could have driven the mare too hard, the horse's assumption of command being a rebellion of sorts.

"George, would you tell us what happened, if you are able?" she asked, turning around to face the boy, cuddled in the arms of his trusted nanny.

George was—conveniently—asleep. Dorinda, now quite confident that his mischief-making had disturbed the horse, reasoned that nevertheless he had been sufficiently punished to spare him further scolding. Master Turner, however, was another chapter in the book, for it was under his trusted supervision that George, still only a small boy, was allowed to ride. If there had been any negligence on the horsemaster's part, Dorinda was not about to let it go unchecked. But she did think it a matter for her father to handle. Turner could retrieve the two mounts from the Guards Stable and return to the townhouse before the earl's arrival home and then be made accountable. As Master Cracker's carriage neared the house, Dorinda could see both her trusted groom and the carriagemaker pacing on the walk, crossing each other's paths time and again.

Peg carried George inside. Still under the power of

"A marvelous notion. George has an influenza. I will notify Peg at once—she'll fret, no doubt."

When the two young ladies next saw each other, it was in their boudoir. The afternoon hours had passed quickly. It was beyond the time for them to dress for dinner.

"Shall I dress the wretch to scare off my unwitting suitor?" Dorie asked aloud.

"No, no, dear sister. All the world knows that it is the beautiful woman who scares off the man. I have noticed that only homely girls marry at a young age. 'Tis best for their parents to make fast work of their matrimonies—before they are past praying for," Winnie said, hoping to lighten her sister's waning spirits.

"Winnie, that is the most cattish observation I have heard you make," Dorinda reprimanded, but could not keep from laughing. "But I have found it true as well."

Dorinda chose a lovely lavender gown with a border of violets embroidered by artful hands. Edwina's selection was a yellow taffeta she had frequently worn, but, as she remarked, "As I doubt we have met tonight's guests before it shall not be lost on them."

After much preening and primping, perfuming and coiffing, the ladies decided amongst them that they were far too beautiful to entice any man who happened into their drawing room. On that joyous commentary, putting all the day's cares and woes behind them, they left the sanctuary of their private suite to join their father downstairs. They had little idea of the length of time they had spent anointing themselves, for their papa was not alone. He was already entertaining his guests.

"Is that not the marquess of Beaumont?" Winnie whispered to her sister while they were still on the stair.

"Yes, I believe it to be him, though we have not had his company for many a year," Dorie answered in a hushed voice.

"But who is that with him? He has his back to us,

5

"I see that you don't remember me, Dorinda. I am Lionel Ridgely," the handsome young man told her.

But Dorinda, recognizing the marquess's son as the man who caused her accident earlier that day, was not even aware of his speaking to her. Nor did she realize that he had relieved his father of the duty of holding her hand. But when Edwina gave her a pinch, Dorinda regained consciousness and drew back sharply.

"And Miss Edwina, I think you were not more than your brother's present age when last we met," he said with great charm.

"I am sorry for ever being at that age," Winnie said flirtatiously, "but I am thankful for this occasion to renew our acquaintance." She batted her eyelashes most coquettishly.

The earl, only too embarrassed at having the wrong daughter respond to the new suitor, begged the little group enter the drawing room for more comfort. Their standing in the foyer seemed to make the situation all the more awkward. He took his younger daughter by the hand and entreated her to sit with him and the marquess on the sofa, leaving the young couple to fend for themselves. Politesse forced Dorinda to share with Lionel the nearby loveseat rather than have him use one of the more

"Whatever is the matter? He is certainly far less displeasing than we imagined—you must admit that," Edwina said, quite taken with him.

"Edwina, he is the perpetrator of this morning's accident, the one who ruined my pink phaeton," Dorie whispered.

"Oh, tsk, tsk," Winnie replied in a tone that said she had already forgiven him, shocking her sister in the extreme.

At the earl's request, Mrs. Garetty placed Dorinda at his right—he being seated at the head of the large mahogany table as was his due—and Lionel at his left. But Peg as usual confused the two and placed the young couple in such a way that permitted Edwina, rather than her sister, to sit next to Lionel. The marquess sat, naturally, at the other head of the rectangular table. At first, the earl was not discomfited by the housekeeper's mistake; he was of the opinion that sitting opposite each other would force one to gaze upon the other and, out of politesse if not desire, would oblige conversation. He did not anticipate that Edwina's close proximity to Lionel would permit her to monopolize him for the duration of the meal.

Dorinda appeared the most annoyed with her sister's behavior. How blatantly she threw herself at the feet of this man, Dorie thought to herself. A man who had so miserably wronged her. But in a corner of her heart she struggled with the possibility that she was a touch jealous of the attention this hauntingly handsome man was showing to Winnie. She found herself, on the one hand, loathing him for both his arrogance and what she thought of as his ineptitude on the carriage path, while, on the other, feeling something she could only describe as the desire to be held close in the strength of his arms. She was ready to slap herself for such a thought, but the two understandable and human female emotions battled each other.

Cook had outdone herself, beginning with the vol-

"What would that be?" she asked her father, never taking her eyes off Lionel.

"A tour of the garden," he said in a firm tone, hoping to, but not succeeding in, getting her full attention.

"Would you like that, Lionel?" Edwina asked him.

"Actually, I am too satiated from the delicious meal to join you, but I am positive my father would heartily say yes to such a kind invitation," Lionel answered adroitly.

"Oh . . ." Edwina said hesitantly, realizing she was trapped.

"A splendid idea, Father," Dorinda said and then, offering her sister a hand, "shall we?"

"Dorinda, I must beg you to stay behind and keep Lionel company. It's past time I look in on my influenzic son. I'm sure the boy's been wondering what could keep his father from his bedside all evening," the earl explained.

Dorinda too was cornered, and thought that the most appropriate course would be to make the best of it by complaining the least about it.

When she and Lionel found themselves alone, she rose from the loveseat they had once again been forced to share, grateful for the opportunity to take a turn about the room. But Lionel was at her side before she knew it.

"How can I tell you how sorry I am that we met under such distressing circumstances? Would it not be possible to begin our friendship anew, starting with tonight instead of today?" he asked in all sincerity.

"I'm afraid that is out of the question," she answered, avoiding those dark eyes. "It is true that we began most unfortunately, but what's done is done and can't be repaired."

"But it can be forgiven," he said, taking her hand

the battle rapidly. When he drew back, she sighed, sorry to be released from his hold and yet grateful for being under her own power again.

He walked to the tea cart and poured a brandy. "Would you like one?" he asked. It was the first time she had been accorded such a privilege.

"I am embarrassed to say I have never tried the liquor," she said modestly.

"Then you shall take a sip of mine," he said and held the glass to her lips.

It warmed her, as had his kiss, but left in no way so sweet an impression.

"I must say I do not care for it much, and it amazes me that men are so fond of—if I may say so—its vile taste," she confessed.

"Sometimes I think that we are not so fond of it, but rather feel obligated to imbibe it, to prove our manhood—'tis a practice I find unnecessary and quite inconclusive, but which, after a time, becomes so accustomed a habit that it's hard to put aside," Lionel said before he took her hand.

They sat on the loveseat again, but no longer each at its opposing far reaches.

"Though I am indeed sorry for our mishap, it will soon be past, forgotten, and all amends made," he said, smiling his boyish grin. "And as I said before, you shall have no qualms about your carriage. It will be repaired and be perhaps even more exquisite than in its former state."

"How so?" she asked.

"I have taken it to Dunbar's, an establishment I find far superior to Cracker's, especially when—"

"Superior to Master Cracker's?" she repeated in disbelief. "He has always been our carriagemaker and has yet to disappoint us."

"I do not mean to call his an inferior house, but Dunbar's is known to be the carriagemaker of most men

always taken it upon myself to see to it that my guests are made to feel welcome. But this exceeds the limits of my temper's measuring cup. I think perhaps you are too close to being all those wretched things I accused you of earlier!" Dorinda pronounced whole-heartedly, and, if she had been just a bit bolder, would have asked him to take back his kiss as well.

They retreated to opposite ends of the room as was the next expected step in any lovers' quarrel.

When the others, who had dispersed to various parts of the house, once again congregated in the drawing room, they viewed this scene, each one differently.

The earl was angered, silently blaming his daughter for the coldness he was sure she displayed in his absence.

The marquess's feelings leaned more toward disappointment that his son had not, to the best of his knowledge and perception, been smitten by Dorinda Tilbury.

Edwina seemed pleased that her sister and the gentleman she herself had taken an immediate fancy to, had not seen fit to bury their differences and adopt a more amicable disposition.

The evening came to an awkward end, with only the marquess speaking to his host, and then only to thank his friend Edmund at great length and to hope they would be reunited sooner than three years hence. Edmund Tilbury shook his hand firmly and said that he could wager on it.

Dorinda and Edwina were busily chatting, comparing their opinions of Lionel, when their father returned to the drawing room.

"Dorinda, what I have to say applies to you, but as I mean to set an example for your sister, she might as well stay, too. It was my great fortune to find Mrs. Garetty with George for no one, until then, saw fit to tell me of his true ailment. Mrs. Garetty, in her excitement over all the events of the day, also explained the mishap with the

of voice. They could not have guessed that it was a manifestation of the fear he had of losing her, as might have been the case in a more disastrous carriage accident, the fear of a future mishap that prompted the earl to so actively plan her marriage. A husband would, he hoped, keep her in check, in the way he no longer could.

"Yes, you will marry Lionel Ridgely before the year is out, before the season is over, I daresay," the earl repeated. And upon that ominous decree, he departed to his suite.

In the hope of cheering her sister, Edwina announced that she had yet another plan. "I will contrive to make Lionel marry *me*," she announced proudly, "since you seem to loathe him so preciously."

Dorinda looked at her sister, but her eyes were not filled with surprise or joy at Winnie's suggestion. Instead, they were possessed by wonder; she was wondering why indeed she did not cotton to her sister's scheme.

to lie in this morning. I don't think you ought to bother her."

"I suppose you're correct," George agreed. "Ever since I was six, they began to object vehemently to my bursting unannounced into their bedchambers, both of them. But perhaps Dorie would not mind if you went up."

"No, I think that totally inappropriate," Lionel said, suppressing laughter. "I doubt Mrs. Garetty would allow me to rest a single foot on the stair. But I will be back, and I will bring with me a picture book or a puzzle to hasten your recuperation and see to it that time does not drag its feet so slowly."

At that, George voiced his wish that Lionel return as soon as it pleased him to do so.

Lionel did return, every day of that week, each time was greeted by George, and told that his sister still refused to come down.

"If I did not know you to be such a nice gentleman," said George, his innocence speaking for him once again, "I would suspect that my sisters were trying to snub you."

"From the mouths of babes . . ." Lionel said to an uncomprehending George. "I don't doubt that is precisely what they have in mind," he said to the boy, in a tone that implied confidentiality, "but I don't understand why it so pleases your sister Edwina who, from what I could ascertain, is so fond of chatting away."

Lionel was about to leave, his visits having become progressively shorter, when sly George, who knew too much of the household goings-on for his own good, asked him to come with him to the garden for a look-see at Winnie's flowers. Not only did they find the flora, but also the younger of his two "indisposed" sisters. Were she not so delighted to see Lionel—despite her sister's admonition that they refuse his visits at all costs—the situation would have been far more awkward. But having stored a

"We must talk," he said, though Dorinda's back was turned to him.

"As you wish," she said.

"Will you face me then?" he asked, approaching her.

She drew in a long breath and turned around. "Shall we sit?"

"Dorinda, I am sorry for the way I behaved the other night. It was unforgivable of me to renew our argument when you had the graciousness to entertain me in your home," he began.

"I've no doubt I provoked you . . . to some extent. I'm equally at fault," she answered truthfully.

"If you cannot find it in your heart to befriend me, we must at least be civil to each other. As you well know, our fathers have conspired to match us and I must follow my parent's direction to court you, no matter how unpleasant you find it, until he is satisfied that our paths are one and the same so that he will return to Tunbridge Wells. We do not have to pretend when we are alone, but we should at least give the illusion of making the effort. Since your father has the same notions as mine, life will be far more pleasant for you as well. Do you understand what I am saying?"

"Yes," she said, "I understand it thoroughly." What she understood was that he cared not a whit for her, that his *mots d'amour* of their last meeting were probably for his father's sake rather than out of any feeling for her. But what did that matter? she wondered. Was it not impossible for her to forgive him? And should she not hope to forget him as well? If only she could loathe him, but his gentle, understanding manner, and his handsome, beguiling features, and the debonair style she had never before seen in a suitor led her to believe it would be impossible to hate him, no matter how much she tried.

Dorinda assumed a collected countenance and told

while she was at Cadfour's for tea with her friend, Lettie Claridge, whom she had encountered while at the Crystal Palace Shoppe, she saw him enter the establishment. Dorinda immediately took to pinching her cheeks to bring back their bloom.

"What has overtaken you?" her little red-haired *amie* asked. "You twitch and quiver as I have never seen. Is there a fly in the air?"

Before Dorinda could answer, Lionel was at their table, kissing her hand, begging to be introduced to her friend.

"Miss Lettie Claridge, allow me to introduce Mr. Lionel Ridgely."

"So pleased to meet you," Lettie said, lowering her eyes. "But why has Dorie not mentioned you to me?"

Dorinda's cheeks no longer required pinching as they blushed a deep red; she longed for a fan. Despite her discomfiture, she couldn't help noticing on her friend's face an expression strangely resembling the one Edwina wore after being introduced to Lionel. It was evident that his handsome looks had the same effect on every lady he met.

"Lionel and I were only recently reacquainted. We were childhood friends, you see," Dorinda recovered enough to say.

"How very interesting," Lettie commented, staring at him all the while.

"I'm sure it is the business of completing all her errands that caused Miss Tilbury to neglect me," he said, with teasing charm. "I have called on her every day, always for nought."

"The preparations for our Ascot home," Dorinda elaborated, wondering why her absences so concerned him. Surely he had made it understood from the start that he was not so exceptionally interested in seeing her as he was in having his father believe it to be so. Most likely it was his excessively gallant nature and nothing more.

for the marchioness's sake, circumstances did not detain his friend Carlton in London for much longer. He succeeded in ruffling Dorinda's defiant feathers, for she promptly left the room without mentioning her afternoon tea.

She regretted, at second thought, quitting her father's company so abruptly. She knew it would have pleased him to learn that she was perhaps not as cold toward the young man as he thought, that *his* coolness was their greatest obstacle. But, finally, she realized such news would have led the earl to confide in his friend, and that was not to be allowed. She would not have the marquess force his son into a marriage he did not want.

It was Edwina who, making discreet inquiries, broached this very subject with her sister.

"Does it still mean nothing to you that Lionel calls here every day?"

"I am convinced that his preoccupation is with you," Dorinda answered, thinking that perhaps today's kindness was to make him appear agreeable as a brother-in-law.

"You care not a whit for him?" Edwina asked, sure in her own mind that he indeed cared for Dorinda. Should she tell her? No, Edwina decided. If Dorie did not care for him, she should not go about putting ideas in her head, sure as she was that she would find it in her own power to bring about a shift in Mr. Ridgely's emotions.

Dorie, for her part wanting to end what she thought of as a one-partnered amour, replied no, hoping if her answer were not presently the truth, it would soon come to be.

Edwina smiled inwardly as she began the stratagem for her campaign to seize Lionel Ridgely's heart.

How perplexing to the observer that so trusting a sisterhood as the one twixt these ladies could be fractured, like their brother's hand, by the arrival of a handsome gentleman.

She prayed he would not see on her face the hurt and disappointment she felt within. She walked to the terrace, a glass of champagne in her hand, and stood motionless, her back to the other guests. This led her father to make an observation.

"It is a pity you do not have two sons," the earl said in an aside to his friend. "And indeed more a pity that I should have two daughters at so close an age."

Dorinda turned around once, only to find Edwina still locked in Lionel's arms. Dorinda went back to counting the stars in the heavens until, after no less than four more dances, she felt someone behind her.

"Your sister can distract a person from even the most important tasks," Lionel told her. "She is a most unique chatterbox."

"You appeared to be her equal," Dorinda replied coolly.

"I fear that seeing me in your sister's arms has not warmed you with any feelings of envy," he said. "I thought I could kindle your interest . . . how come you to be so aloof a young woman?" he asked boldly.

Dorinda looked up at him with lovelorn eyes. "Indifferent? It is you who are indifferent, showing the same quality of attentiveness to every lady. Of course you are pleasant and kind, cordial . . . but it is plain that I am mere diversion for you. Or a way to ease your father's concerns."

"Dorinda, I said those things because I thought that was what you wanted to hear. We have known each other too long for me to be cold to you. How could you believe such a thing?"

"Your very actions speak for you," Dorinda said, threatening to raise her voice, but remembering where they were.

"My act—" here he stopped abruptly. "No, I shall not let you draw me into another argument as to who is the culprit. You did that once before, and so succeeded in

of so eligible an admirer, both when he called on her at Park Lane and when they saw each other at the many parties around town. But with the family's departure for Ascot growing so dangerously close, she grew sad at the thought of losing his company for the coming months. That unhappy note was on the verge of interjecting itself into the conversation, but on one particular visit, nothing could have marred her joy. It was the day he returned her pink phaeton, repaired and freshly painted, its luster, as he had promised, far surpassing its original condition.

"Lionel, shall we take a ride together through the park?" she asked, grateful that Edwina was ignorant of his arrival and still sequestered in her chamber.

"Riding in the same coach is the only safe fashion for us," he said, giving her cause for laughter.

She thought that social pretentions would forbid her to conduct the carriage when in the company of a gentleman, but Lionel was not a prissy. As soon as they turned the phaeton onto the East carriage road, he gave her command of the vehicle. She was certain now that she could love him, both for himself and for the way he made her feel.

Lionel surprised her again some time later when he seized the reins, and drew the horses to a halt. He turned toward her, those dark eyes captivating her with their intent. Before she could protest, he took her in his arms and kissed her. She closed her eyes and was lost in a sea of new desire.

It was Lionel who separated them and began, remarkably, to apologize for his forwardness.

"I had best take you home," he told her, and she sensed his regret.

"Why are you sorry for your show of affection?" she asked, placing her hand on his arm.

"I oft forget that you are a proper young lady of London and a childhood friend as well," he replied cautiously.

treaty of her story that Dorinda, all but her eyes shielded by the *billet du jour,* caught sight of Lionel entering the establishment with a raven-haired beauty on his arm.

Dorinda's heart sank. Though her good sense tried to tell her there must be a satisfactory explanation, her eyes read another tale in his actions. While she pretended to listen to her friend's speech, her attention was held by Lionel and the woman whose hands he so tenderly caressed. Dorinda saw the woman sob at one moment, rest her head on Lionel's shoulder afterward, and then laugh at something Lionel said.

Dorinda toyed with her nuncheon—a cold collation of beef and legumes, while her friend, needing this fuel to continue her discourse, ate ravenously. Penelope was undeterred by Dorinda's lack of conversation—she was content to supply it entirely. When she did ask after Dorinda's news, it was just an afterthought, and Dorinda replied that there was nothing to tell. Penelope took this as a signal to renew her tirade. Dorinda, had she been more in control of her wits, would have been grateful for not having to participate; but all she wanted to do was go home and bury her face in her pillow.

More sadly for Dorinda, it was not the solace of her room that awaited her, but her anxious papa who called to her from his favorite seat in the drawing room.

"Dorinda," he said, "come and sit. It has been far too long since we have talked."

Dorinda thought the subject of Lionel a far too recently broached topic at the Tilbury house. She was not looking forward to answering renewed inquiries on the progress of their courtship. But she was ever the dutiful daughter and sat down by his side.

"Dorinda, it distresses me to think that we are to quit London for upward of three months with nothing having been decided between you and Lionel. Is it your coldness that has caused this stagnation?" he asked.

her own lovesickness. She kissed him at this curious interval and quit the room herself.

Left alone in the drawing room, the earl threw up his hands. "Daughters! What is a father to do with them but try to marry them off?"

"Peg, dearest—" she began, but her surrogate mother stopped her with a wave of her hand.

"Now don't be givin' me any stories of a lost appetite. I'll have none of it. Though the earl may be my master, I tell you he shan't upset my Dorie that she can't take her dinner," she said, and took a bedroom gown from Dorie's armoire. "I can still remember the days when I'd dress you and Winnie for bed after your bath. You'd scamper around this room as though you were of the same birth, so alike were you. It does my heart good to care for you as though you was a little one again," Peg said, little knowing that Dorinda was thinking a similar thought.

Yes. To be a young one again, free of the pressures of encroaching adulthood.

"And will you brush my hair as you did when I was less defiant?" Dorinda asked, as her beloved "nanny" was about to leave her to her supper.

Dorinda, turning her back to Peg to facilitate the task, sat on her bed and faced the window. With the mother-of-pearl brush, Mrs. Garetty began to coif those long blond tresses. Dorinda stared up to the sky, now deep colors of azure as the day drew to its close, and wondered what the heavens had prescribed for her.

The one thing not in store for her was a visit from Lionel Ridgely the next day, or the next. On both occasions she sent her regrets to Miss Claridge, whom she had promised to visit once more before leaving for Ascot. She was determined to give Lionel every opportunity to explain his absences as well as the scene she had witnessed at Lillywhite's. But this was not to be. She stayed home for nought. Though she attempted to complete a painting, she could not even concentrate fully enough to compose her palette. There was much wringing of the hands and pacing back and forth. She would sit on the divan and rise an instant later; she would walk toward the pantry,

with you then, and take with you my prayers for your success," he offered.

If only there hadn't been a certain agitation in Lionel's voice, the marquess would not have been left to wonder again whether his son was on the verge of entering into another scrape.

The marquess was still pondering this question when Edmund Tilbury joined him.

"I am distressed to find you still in London!" was the earl's greeting.

"Truth be told!" the marquess snarled.

"I am grateful for your company, Carlton. It is only that I had hoped by this time our two children would have come to the sterling realization that they are perfectly suited to each other—despite their bickering," Edmund confided.

"I understand perfectly . . . I wonder if we would have been more successful launching Edwina," the marquess suggested.

"Do you have it on Lionel's authority that he prefers Winnie? A substitution might very well be arranged," the earl said, as though these two were as perfectly suited as well.

"No, not at all. My son does not confide in me in the least. It is only that they appear to get along famously. Surely you have noticed the same."

"Appearances mean nothing," the earl replied with conviction. "Winnie's behavior is due to her inexperience. A young girl's head is bound to be turned by the first handsome man she meets." His reasoning far exceeded the power that said daughter had attributed to him. "I think it is but a matter of time, for when I talked to Dorinda about your son the other evening, the girl was moved to tears. That, to me, has but one explanation. The girl's taken with him! She is as anxious for him to come to scratch as we are."

have it accepted and carried out," the marquess insisted.

"The stipulation is accepted," Edmund said, holding out his hand. "You have a bargain." He hoped silently that the bargain he had made with his daughter, nearly two months before, would be met as successfully as this.

"In that case, I refuse to go!"

Having put full credence in his assumption that Dorinda's heart had grown tender for Lionel Ridgely, the earl had returned home that evening and wasted no time in announcing what he was sure would be a most pleasing surprise. It was not. He never imagined the sharpness of her reaction.

"And I tell you, you will come with us to Ascot, or suffer the consequences," the earl retorted hotly.

"Father, I have always considered Ascot, and this townhouse, mine as well as yours. I never supposed that you would take it upon yourself to make my sister and brother and me suffer the company of unwanted guests, whom we are obliged to entertain, without being considerate enough to ask us first," Dorinda voiced.

"Daughter, as you say, these are *my* homes and I see no reason why I should be obliged to ask you or your eight-year-old brother for consent in my actions! I will warn you once again that you will face severe consequences if you do not obey my wishes and be hostess to my friends, friends who, I might add, have been friends of yours since your birth!" the earl retaliated.

"And of what consequences do you speak so persistently?" Dorinda asked, knowing them full well.

"While you continue to live in our home, though past your majority, you are under my wing. If you insist on refusing my guidance, I will turn you out of this house, be it into the arms of a husband or not. And you will see how cruel that world can be . . . and how loving this one

"Daughter, that is a question you would not even ask of me. As the marquess gave no further explanation, it would certainly have been even more out of place for me to ask either gentleman of their private affairs," he cautioned.

"I am sorry, Father, but I cannot suffer the company of Lionel Ridgely, knowing that it would be for every waking hour of each day," she said. Though she longed to see him again, it would be impossible to be content, believing he was interested in another.

"Daughter, that is something you must acclimate yourself to, for it is doubtful—unless you wish a miserable existence—that as man and wife you will not live under a common roof!"

"Father, I am as vehement as you in upholding my side of the argument. I tell you one last time that I will not be accompanying you, and I will not say another word."

Dorinda turned to leave his study where, away from the most frequented sector of the house, they had thought to have this discussion in private, but found herself face to face with George.

"I will not go if you do not," he pronounced boldly. "You will need a man in the house and that will be me."

The humor of this was lost to their father.

"Dorinda, I will not have you disrupt this household any further," he insisted before stalking out of the room.

Dorie hugged the boy, pressing him as close to her as she could.

"George, you are the most loving and wonderful brother a girl could hope to have. I am deeply moved by your kind and thoughtful offer, but as father said, this argument is between him and me. I could not suffer to let you in the midst of it. It is to him that you owe your first

not bear to speak. She left the house last, kissing Dorinda goodbye for the third time.

"Your groom will look after you," she told the girl, "until you join us." She didn't wait for Dorinda's answer.

Dorinda went out to the garden and sat on the white wrought-iron divan whose satin pillows had been removed indoors the day before. She wanted to curse Lionel Ridgely for tearing her family apart, her heart apart. She would pen a note to her mother's relations as soon as she retired, and she and Bucky would begin the journey in a day or two. She was happy to see the groom, who seemed to be at her side at every crisis, when he appeared in the doorway.

"I am planning to visit some relations in Liverpool," she told him. "You will have to see to the renting of a coach."

"The pink phaeton is available, Miss. It could take the journey with no problem," he said, surprising her.

"My father did not take the carriage?"

"His new carriage arrived this very morn, a regal black coach—from Dunbar's you know, at Mr. Lionel's suggestion."

Dorinda burst into a torrent of tears and Bucky strained to think of what he had said to cause such a reaction. He tried to calm her with words.

"You needn't feel too bad for Cracker . . . and Dunbar's is so far improved, as Mr. Lionel said. Your father agreed with Mr. Lionel when he saw the coach—I think Mr. Lionel a good sort, and he's greatly fond of you . . ." When Bucky realized that he had produced the opposite of the desired effect—an even more powerful deluge, he stopped his speech.

"I can't bear it if you say his name one more time," she said, still sobbing.

"Master Cracker?" he asked.

She shook her head vehemently—no.

him again. In the end, she determined to win his affections.

She decided to follow Bucky's plan, though it might mean only one last rendez-vous with Lionel: If he did not come true with her, she would ask him to end the charade and tell his father that he was not going to propose. Surely if he had shown her any part of his nature, it was that he would not be bullied by his parent. He had it in his power to stop the feuding between Dorinda and her father—if not by marriage then by reason.

"Bucky, as soon as my packing is finished, we will leave," she said, preparing to quit the garden.

"Mrs. Garetty has already seen to that for you," he told her quickly.

"Peg has packed my trunks?"

"Yes, Miss; I suppose she took a notion that you'd be traveling to Ascot after all," he explained, chuckling.

"Dear Peg," Dorinda said, thinking of the many years of kindness and devotion the woman had showed her family. "She knows me too well. . . . As soon as I have changed my gown, then."

With a smile on his face, the young boy set to the task of placing those trunks in the carriage.

The sparkling pink phaeton was at the ready when Dorinda descended in that brilliant pink gown her sister had given her on her birthday. As a surprise for Ascot, Edwina had had a parasol fashioned in the same material, and now Dorinda opened it against the bright June sunlight.

Bucky offered to help her into the rear of the carriage but she explained that she would rather sit with him at the reins. It had been many days since she had left the house, much less ridden in her beloved carriage. She knew that the great road leading out of London was not the same as park paths, but she assured him it would not

8

Bucky was at her side in a moment. Together they carried Lionel to her phaeton, where he was rested across the leather banquette. He was still bleeding from the gash on his forehead, and Dorinda did not hesitate to bandage it with her pink voile shawl, folded in thirds. She motioned to Bucky to take her linen handkerchief, and all those he could find in her purse, and to soak them through with water from the bottles they had brought with them. Thankfully the water was still cool. She wrung the linen thoroughly and made a compress for Lionel's head, applying it with pressure, hoping to stay the bleeding. But it was not the gash that worried her.

Lionel had lapsed into unconsciousness.

"Bucky, he is in want of medical attention," she told the equally concerned groom. "We must travel ahead to the nearest village and seek out their physician or he will be lost to us."

Bucky agreed. "That would be the best course, but I should like to hitch Mr. Lionel's horses to our carriage. It will take but a moment, and if not, they will surely die of thirst in this sun, or be stolen."

"Of course," Dorinda said, grateful that he had thought of the mounts. "What of the carriage?"

"I'm sorry to say that Dunbar's work no longer

finding him a sign of their being destined for each other? There was no more she had to know.

When the carriage came to a halt, Bucky announced that they were in the town of Dorking. He had asked a farmer pushing his cart of produce to recommend an inn where they might put up; he would leave the recommendation of a physician to a more trustworthy authority.

The innkeeper of the Dorking Royal Inn, Mrs. Skeetles, informed Bucky that she had but one large room to let.

"This town is the natural resting post for those grand souls traveling to Ascot, boy, and all my rooms are promised *in advance*," she said reproachfully. "But, as I've said, I have one room left—nothing fancy, mind you . . ."

"I'm certain it will do nicely," he informed her, and gave the names of its occupants as Mr. and Mrs. Lionel Ridgely.

When he told Dorinda of the single vacancy, she told the groom not to think twice upon it.

"We must accept whatever lodgings are available, for Lionel's sake. There's no time to worry about appearances," she said, unaware that he had had them married to avoid just such a worry.

After seeing his mistress and the patient to their room—and quite an appearance they made, carrying the robust-physiqued man with the help of only one other—Bucky asked Mrs. Skeetles for the name of a reputable physician.

"But you're a fortunate scamp," she told him. "We've one of the Harley Street men here, yes, comes up every year for our quail. Did I tell you our quail are amongst the finest in all the kingdom? Raise 'em ourselves, we do."

"Pleased to hear it, ma'am, but the physician . . ." Bucky pleaded. "Could you tell me his name and where I might find him?"

of his diagnosis, but she was more relieved when the doctor expertly dressed Lionel's wound.

"I will leave the jar with you. Apply the salve as you change the bandage each morning. Do not be concerned if you see fresh blood on the gauze. The cut must cleanse itself. If it becomes more profuse, apply pressure, as I can see you did before," he instructed.

"Thank you, Doctor," she said, extending her hand.

"Do try the quail here—it is of an excellent caliber," he said as he left. "And hearty congratulations!"

"Yes, thank you," Dorinda murmured, her nerves set on edge once again.

Bucky was about to slip from the room when he heard his mistress call his name.

"Miss?"

"Bucky, why did Dr. Trepperwood address me as Mrs. Ridgely?"

"Must be what Mrs. Skeetles said was your name," he answered sheepishly.

"And what would have given her such an idea?" she asked impatiently, losing all trace of her calm reserve.

"I must own up to the crime, Mrs. Ridg—Miss Tilbury. But it was our very own Mr. Lionel who instructed me. He said the best groom was the one who has the best master—or mistress. Appearances, don't you know," he said, his freckles fading into a blush.

Dorinda was satisfied with his explanation, and even fancied the tale to be true, if but for a moment. Indeed, she felt like a wife watching over her ailing husband. But it was not a fib they could pretend at for long, however much she might have enjoyed it. What if Dr. Trepperwood should take it in his head to congratulate her father upon seeing him in Ascot, she wondered. She could only hope to be the first of the two to arrive there and explain the situation. He was certain to understand, she concluded, and was able to set her mind to rest.

"I thank you for all your concern, Bucky. You are

body on the divan so that she might sleep. But no more than two hours passed before she returned to her vigil.

Dorinda was unfailing in her care of Lionel, seeing to his every need, though he was not able to voice a single one. When Bucky persuaded her to rest that afternoon, it could not have been called sleep. She stirred every few minutes, thinking she had heard Lionel call for her. After she woke complaining of a nightmare, of seeing Lionel on the road but not being able to help him, she decided she would sooner fight off sleep than succumb to the demons in her dreams. And so she sat, holding Lionel's hand every minute, until he woke, at last, the next day.

"Dorinda."

"Yes, Lionel, I'm here," she said, as she took his hand.

His dark eyes sought out her lovely face and she felt his hand tighten around hers.

"What happened?" he asked. "I can only remember losing control of the horses. The carriage—it was going too fast . . ."

"I can only guess that you were thrown from the carriage as it toppled off the road. We found you on the nearby field, unconscious," she explained, painfully reliving the moment.

"We? I thought you and father had already left for Ascot. I was hoping to overtake you on the road," he said in a weak voice.

"My groom, Bucky, and I were traveling to Ascot some hours after our parents had left," she said, without giving any reason. "We were in the pink phaeton."

"The phaeton brings us together once again," he said softly, squeezing her hand again.

"Please do not strain to talk, I beseech you. You need quiet to regain your strength," she said tenderly.

"At least tell me the time of day, be it night or morn. Indeed, what date is it? I feel as though I have had

Bucky poured him a brandy, which seemed to lessen, if not relieve, the pain.

"Tell me then, Dorinda—or should I say 'wife'?—did you contrive to have us married in the midst of my unconsciousness? What primitive tactics for securing a husband," he teased her. "It must have been at my parent's instigation."

"Have no fear of it. You are the way I first found you," she said blushing. "Eligible and egotistical."

"Then how comes that rapscallion of a groom to call us such?" he asked.

"It is a scheme of the lad's—to maintain 'appearances', as he calls it. A word he undoubtedly learned at your side," she admonished him.

"Then it was rightly done," he said, commending the proud boy.

"Shall we leave it to him to explain to your parent and mine?" she asked.

But Lionel could not answer. He had lapsed into sleep, not one of unconsciousness, but of recovery.

"I hope your piece of mischief does not backfire," she warned Bucky. "What we have gained in Dorking, we stand to lose in Ascot."

Dorinda was convinced that they should quit the town at the earliest possible convenience and hurry to Ascot before both families descended upon them. She told Bucky that they would leave in the morning, if Lionel was able to walk. For the first time during the Dorking sojourn, she began to feel peculiar about her close proximity to Lionel Ridgely, especially during the nighttime hours. Her pure conscience told her there was nothing wrong in her tending to him, though there was a certain impropriety in their sharing a room, now that he had regained his faculties. She laughed when she thought of his reaction to such a judgment. He would scorn such pretentious notions and find nothing wrong in their sequestering.

was four days ago. Though I refuse to play the invalid, I will take every moment with more thought and less speed."

"That it is the only attitude to adopt, as your carriage was ruined beyond repair. You will content yourself with riding well inside my phaeton, for you are at my mercy," she said to him, with newfound daring. She was every bit a match for his brand of intrigue.

He took her hand and kissed it. "There is no place fairer."

"I was not so sure of that when you quit London without a word," she said, her curious heart prompting her to introduce a subject her manners would not have otherwise allowed.

"I must explain that—" he began, but raised his hands to cradle his head, hoping this would stop the renewed cacophony of sound that tormented him from within.

"There will be time for explanation later," she said, "when you are more fully recovered."

The conversation en route to Ascot consisted in the main of Dorinda inquiring, every quarter hour, whether Lionel would be most comfortable with a pillow behind his head or under his feet, or perhaps with no pillow at all. She fussed over him until he fell asleep, his fatigue the victor in the battle with the bumpy road. It was a long, arduous journey, and night had fallen before they arrived at the graystone country manor of the earl of Balmoral.

As soon as the inhabitants heard the clapping of horses in the cobblestone drive, they emerged, one and all, bearing lanterns to light the way.

"Oh, Lionel! We were all terribly distressed!" Edwina said, throwing her arms around him.

"But you are all in one piece," George said, disappointed.

"You must excuse the child," Winnie told Lionel, though she was not so far removed from that appellation.

"To tell you true, Lionel and I are not married." All but Edwina let out a great cry of disappointment. "Lionel was not fully conscious until this very morning, and for want of a better nurse, I stayed at his side for the duration. For the sake of propriety, Bucky dubbed us man and wife to all at the Inn. You see, there was but one lodging available and we could not move Lionel any farther—the situation was completely innocent," she said, unable to sound less guilty.

"Innocent?" her father echoed with disbelief.

"He could not be left alone at the mercy of a child like Bucky. And he was unconscious, Father. But I do not think he is so well recovered that we should presume upon his good health," she said, hoping to be alone when her father vented his anger. "It's time Mrs. Garetty showed him his room."

The marquess led his son up the stairs, with Edwina, ever solicitous, and George tailing behind. Dorinda was wont to retire to her own room, but her father put his firm hand on her shoulder.

"Innocent or nay, your conduct has too much an air of disrepute. I care not of the opinion all of Dorking has, but the one entertained by Carlton Ridgely and his son. Your intimacies leave you no choice but to marry the man posthaste, before the true circumstances of these past days are common knowledge to all, from Ascot to London. I will not have my daughter's reputation 'innocently' dragged through the mire," he informed her, in no uncertain terms. "You will commit yourselves one to the other before the races are done."

"Would you have had me leave Lionel in the road rather than risk some fools' talk? What a fine specimen of husband he would have been then," she taunted him.

"If you tended him with such devoted care, it could only be due to tender feelings for the young man. Though you are an admirable creature who is concerned with the plight of one and all, to take such pains to sit at a man's

99

Dorinda was not unnerved by her father's ranting. She had escaped his plans to date, and was certain she could continue to do so in the future. But she was nevertheless overwrought by her labors of the past days, and was anxious to gain the comfort of her own room. A loud, incessant knocking at the front door prevented her from doing so . . . indefinitely.

Mrs. Garetty, always the last asleep in the manor, opened the door as her mistress reached it.

"Where is my son? I demand to know!" A woman, flamboyantly dressed in black and red, said as she led a parade of unknowns into the Tilbury home.

"Until you tell me who you might be, Madam, I can't presume to know who's your son," Mrs. Garetty said, unfamiliar with such rudeness.

"I am the marchioness of Beaumont," she announced, pounding her hand upon her breast. "And I have come to see my son. Will you tell me where he is now, or shall I search every room?" she asked, looking from Peg to Dorinda.

Dorinda and Peg exchanged expressions of amazement. Was this the poor ailing wife Carlton Ridgely had spoken of with such tenderness and compassion? The look on Mrs. Garetty's face said she wondered whether it was possible for the marquess to have two wives. When she saw the startled man on the stair behind her, she knew it would only be a moment before she had her answer.

the only one I trust to examine my child, and a man I have the utmost confidence in. Will you then, Peg Garetty, show us to my Lionel's room?"

"Yes, your ladyship," Peg answered. "It is just up the stairs."

With the doctor in tow, she followed Peg, leaving another woman, who was indeed a stranger to Dorinda, standing awkwardly in the foyer.

"We have not been introduced. I am Dorinda Tilbury," she said, trying to put her at ease.

"I am a friend of the marchioness," the lady said, "Countess Alicia Mongrieg. Fiona was so distraught this morning, I thought it best to accompany her, not realizing, until now, how thoughtless that was."

"Yes, the doctor would have been sufficient," the marquess said coarsely. It was apparent that he did not count himself among the countess's friends.

"You are entitled to your opinion," she said, aware of his feelings—or lack of any—for her. "But I am here nonetheless, and will try to be as useful as possible."

"You are welcome, of course," Dorinda said, her mother's child in all matters of social politesse.

The countess was a woman lovely in appearance, still quite youthful looking though Dorinda guessed her age to be close to that of her own father. Her eyes were most captivating, her features still as striking as those of a woman half her age.

By this time, the rest of the Tilbury family, including George who was most easily awakened by any form of intrigue, had assembled in the foyer, and were anxiously awaiting an explanation for all the footsteps that had gone past their respective rooms.

"Father, this is Countess Mongrieg, a friend of the marchioness, who is now participating in an examination of her son aided by her personal physician," Dorinda said, accurately describing the chain of events.

"I see," the earl said, seeing no one save the count-

But until I am certain of Lionel's feelings, I will not be so presumptuous as to voice my own," Dorinda confessed.

At these words, Edwina's heart began to pound heavily within her breast, and she could hardly move to take in a breath of air. Was she undone? "How do you mean, Sister," she asked, "for since the day you first met Lionel you have been vehemently complaining of your dislike for him?"

"Winnie, you know so little in matters of love . . . but because you are my sister, I will tell you. I am deeply fond of Mr. Ridgely, more so than I have ever been of any man. He is kind and understanding, not at all stuffy and boorish, as are most of the men father chooses to introduce me to. There is an aliveness in Lionel's voice that is so forthright and open that one cannot help but fall under his charming spell," Dorinda explained.

"I cannot believe I hear these words upon your lips, where only a few weeks ago found such oaths uttered on Lionel's head that I would not dare repeat them. I cannot believe that you have deceived me so cruelly," Edwina said, a never before heard hostility in her voice. "I never thought my sister would seek to thwart me in matters of the heart as you do now. To purposefully tell me you loathe Lionel and then, once the strings of my heart have been tuned, to renounce the hatred for fondness. I will not have it!" she screamed on the threshold of a tantrum, so unbecoming to her years.

"But Edwina, my love, whatever can prompt you to speak with such harshness in your voice? Am I not the sister closest to your heart? Do I now have to suppose that you will take it in your head to fancy those who come calling on me? I cannot imagine what in Lionel's behavior ever prompted the notion that he could be a suitor of yours. Edwina, you have not yet had your come-out, are not yet eligible. How can these shocking words I hear come from such innocent lips as yours?" Dorinda asked, trying to understand the folly that had overtaken her sister.

the description "romantic" had ever transpired between them. In fact, the two men were more devoted one to the other than either was to her.

Arthur, the Baron Hapsley, was the son of a relation to the Montgomery Hapsleys of Plymouth, and to that he owed his greatest debt, family income sufficient to preclude his choosing a career that might have added significance to his existence. He was a tall twig of a gentleman, with brownish hair and a nearly white complexion that might look Godsent on a woman, but happened to be devilishly morbid on this man. His dull blue eyes did little to improve his physical countenance. But he was a kind, soft-hearted man, taken to providing for all the stray cats in the countryside he loved. Dorinda had thought he would make a wonderfully practical husband, the type who would let his wife hold the reins.

Mr. Felix Horatio was a short, rather stubby figure, whose pale blond hair and complexion threatened to blend him imperceptibly into the horizon, were it not for his ruddy nose. He occupied a cottage, not far from the Hapsley home, left him by his departed father. He too chose not to be gainfully employed for his living, but preferred to spend his time gossiping with Lord Hapsley, and tending to a garden kept alive and verdant all the year 'round with the help of a hothouse.

There was a note of familiarity that Dorie felt with them. She had come to know them a little better each year since . . . she could not remember when. It seemed that Ascot meant Arthur-and-Felix as much as it did grooming the horses, wearing the family colors, and throwing the Tilbury bash, the crowning event of the week, a party that was renowned throughout the countryside, and to which an invitation was the most coveted piece of post.

"Have I told you that Viscount Dalrymple has left his wife and children to take up with a bar wench?" Felix asked her.

once. My father's guests will be highly insulted to think you suspect their innocence," she pronounced with a pout. "I am ashamed of both of you for your heart-rendering outburst."

"Oh, Dorinda, pray forgive me," Felix said, taking her hand.

"And me as well," said Arthur, taking the other.

"The last thing we wish to do is invoke your displeasure," both said nearly in unison, and began babbling anew about the Ascot goings-on.

They so entertained Dorinda, that when Lionel walked out, unobserved, onto the patio, he saw a most pleased expression on her face. Seeing her hands in theirs, he drew all the wrong, impossible conclusions, however naturally.

"A fine scene this is!" said a female voice. The marchioness had walked up behind her son.

"Oh dear!" cried Felix.

"On my!" cried Arthur.

Dorinda rose to make the necessary introductions, hoping to stay any further outcries. After the completion of this task, both gentlemen surprised Dorinda by announcing that they would take their leave. They no doubt wished to discuss the picture Lady Ridgely presented in her crimson and violet dressing gown.

"We shall see you at the Spreaklingers'," Arthur said, reminding Dorinda of the tea which officially started the racing festivities.

"And have I mentioned that my cousin Roddy will be in attendance? You will adore him, I am certain," Felix insisted.

"I would be honored to meet him," Dorinda said to please her friends, wondering if she could stand the adoration of a trio.

"Until the Spreaklingers' then," they said to Dorinda and left the patio, arm in arm.

Dorinda was about to explain her peculiar friends

alliance. But those events need never travel further than these ears."

Upon that note, the marchioness left her to ponder the outcome of her arrival.

It was not enough that their fathers conspired against Dorinda and Lionel by plotting their union. Now they would have yet another dissenting voice to add to the melée.

But Dorinda took heart and made up her mind to be utterly bright and cheerful. She was overjoyed to find the room she now shared with Winnie unoccupied when she went to don her tea dress, and was thankful for small favors such as this.

She put on the fanciful yellow and emerald robe, provocatively designed, though its chief function was to represent the Balmoral colors. A matching parasol added just the right dash of country charm to the reflection she saw of herself in the cheval glass. Her blond curls were appropriately pulled up into a neat bun with tiny ringlets gracefully framing her face. She was pleased with the image.

She knew that Lionel would not be attending the tea, his mother's physician having proclaimed him too weak, but she also knew that she would be able to parade her new fashion before him as she quit the house. It would not cause a relapse, she thought devilishly, for him to suffer the sting of jealousy that was all too at home in her own heart. Perhaps it would ripen his more admirable feelings for her.

When she descended, she was given word by Peg that Edwina suffered with an undefined malaise, and had decided to remain at home.

"I see," Dorinda said, but could not help thinking that the true illness which had stricken the girl was merely her immature infatuation with Lionel. She found them in the garden, seated in chairs placed side by side.

Dorinda cleared her throat to gain their attention.

The afternoon sky was a crisp, clear blue, unbroken by any cloud. Dorinda looked over the various patchworks of tended fields in the distance. Though most homes in the wealthy area belonged to the nobility of England, there was an occasional baron or even viscount who still believed in harvesting from the earth her nourishment.

Dorinda knew each of the grand estates by name— "Country Timberlane," "Clearwater Ponds," "The Three Crests of Dimesdale" (the fabulous home of Lord and Lady Pericles), to name but a few. As a child, she had played with the offspring of all these country cousins, together they had been taught riding and swimming in the summer, attended dancing school in the fall upon their return to London. Now, the young men were off to college or the wars; the young ladies, many far younger than she, had settled into homes of their own. As she rode, she dreamed, for the first time since childhood, of the day she would bid adieu to her ancestral home to lay the foundation of one brand new.

When she arrived at the Spreaklingers', she saw that her father's carriage was parked alongside others, though none so new and shiny black. A Spreaklinger groom aided her from the carriage, unable to conceal the look of surprise at the sight of so tender and fragile a lady daring to blister her soft hands on the leather reins. Dorinda smiled. To answer the questioning look would have been out of place. Though she might have eased her defenses on one or two occasions with her own groom Bucky, to answer the inquisitiveness of a peer's servant was, according to the laws set down long ago by others, out of the realm of acceptability.

The roses and the carnations in the Spreaklingers' four-tiered garden had bloomed, Dorie was sure, on their owners' command. There was a sensuality in the air made heady by the aromas of verbena, jasmine, and lilac imported from France; they intermingled with the bush flowers and gave the party an air of fantasy. Though called a

osity. "I wear these bracelets because of their awesome beauty and to honor his memory."

"Was it not fortunate that the marchioness recovered sufficiently to make the journey to Ascot?" Edmund Tilbury asked, stating his own opinion within his question.

"Yes indeed, Father," Dorinda replied dutifully. She wondered whether this woman who so captivated him could turn his attentions toward a marriage of his own. Nay, she thought, it was ridiculous, premature, and yet she had never seen that expression of adoration on his face. And too, the countess had distracted him sufficiently for him to put the subject of his daughter's marriage completely out of his thoughts.

"Where have the Ridgelys gotten off to, Father?" she asked, interrupting his fascination with the countess's eyes.

"I think they have retreated to the arbor, to renew an old acquaintance," the countess said, aiding her inarticulate escort.

At that very moment an old friend of the Tilbury family approached them. It was the earl of Darcy, who now made his home in Ascot, but who was once her father's very able equal in Parliament. Lawrence Wentworth, the earl's given name, provided the only wager his friend Edmund accepted each year; they had bet against each other's horses for more than twenty.

"Dorie, you are more lovely each time I see you," he said kindly. "But where is your fetching sister, Winnie?" Do not tell me she has stayed behind in London—she always delighted in rooting for my entries."

"Do not think it, Lord Wentworth. She is at home, with a slight indisposition," Dorinda explained.

"I do hope it will clear itself in time for her to witness my prized 'Lady Anna's Garter' win the title," he said, poking a bit of fun at Lord Tilbury.

"Is that the name of the mule?" Edmund Tilbury

blond stranger reached their little party, "allow me to present my cousin Roddy."

"Short for Roderick, don't you know," Arthur interjected.

"The Viscount Farleigh, to be accurate," Felix amended. "But Roddy to all his friends."

"Miss Tilbury, it is an honor to make your acquaintance. Though we meet now for the first time, I feel as though I have known you all my life. My cousin Felix writes often of the excitement you bring with you to Ascot," Roderick told her, after kissing her hand.

"But how can it be that we have never before met?" Dorinda asked, sorry for the fact. "My family sojourns in Ascot every summer, and I have yet to see you here. Pray do not say you visit only in winter."

"I am afraid it is only the rare occasion that brings me from my ancestral seat in Sunderland. This visit is due to a piece of family business that could not be fully tended to through the post," he explained. "If I had but known that one so lovely as you takes up residence here each spring, I should have found it in my power long ago to make the journey south."

To say that Dorinda was surprised at the gentlemanly charms of Felix's cousin would not be description enough; she was shocked, indeed taken aback that close relations could beget two offspring so different.

When Dorinda suggested that perhaps their paths had crossed in London, Roderick was forced to deny the possibility.

"It has only been two years since my father passed his title on to me. I spent the twenty-five preceding years in wholly uninteresting pursuits in the northern countryside, completely uninterested in the business affairs of my family. And the larger part of the past two years has been spent on the sea; I have been voyaging between England and the Scandinavian countries with

counts of personal exploits, that she lost all sense of the hour and all memory of having thought to return home prematurely. When it was the appropriate time to quit the Spreaklingers', it was Roderick who requested the honor of escorting her home. She accepted most heartily.

It was not until they reached Balmoral House that Dorinda's mind hit upon Lionel Ridgely. She invited Roderick into the commons room, but before the others arrived in the earl's carriage, Dorinda slipped to the patio doors and saw, with desperate eyes, Lionel and Winnie sitting side by side, as she had left them.

Dorinda turned to Roderick and asked, "Shall we venture outside? Perhaps you will consent to tell me more about your proposed voyage to the Ukraine," she suggested, as she led her new friend out to the terrace.

The change in Lionel's complacent expression to one of questioning disapproval pleased Dorinda greatly. She and Roderick stopped only to make the briefest introductions and continued on to the duck pond.

Dorinda and Roddy, as he insisted she call him, conversed until the blazing sun gave way to the faint image of the moon rising in the blue-purple sky. He regretfully took his leave when Dorinda explained that she must withdraw. Indeed it was well past the time for her to dress for supper. And, as she thought again of that questioning look on Lionel's face, would have invited the Viscount Roddy to stay to sup, were it not highly improper, his being a stranger to her father.

Were Dorinda not truly intrigued by this man, such a thought would not have entered her mind. She was not the sort of woman who would deliberately bring a man to jealousy with the aid of another, who would seek a man's love through his jealousy. Entertaining the viscount was as much for her own pleasure as for the effect it would have on Lionel. She was satisfied when he promised to see her on the morrow, at the opening festivities of the racing tourney.

10

On the morrow, Dorinda kept her promise to herself. She visited the stables to see her "pets," both to reassure the horses she rode for pleasure and to lend encouragement to those entered in the races. The thoroughbreds of her childhood years had bred offspring that were stronger and faster; she admired one and all.

Tommy Winslow and his younger brother Bobby, the children of their horse trainer, were washing down London's Pride and Nell's Bell, two of the most prized fillies. In a nearby stall, Daring Lady, who had not run these past three years, was nursing her new foal, destined to be a champion. The old horse knew Dorinda and let her pet and coddle the offspring. Dorinda gave Daring's mane a tousle and offered her a barley treat from a pouch.

At the far end of the stable were the horses ridden for pleasure, and Dorinda bid good morning to all before she returned to Golden Sunset. The horse had been a gift from Eloise Tilbury—the last. Though she had since acquired others, Sunset was the only one she rode. The mare was almost human in her moods—the gaiety in her step, the devotion to her mistress, the warm look in her dark brown eyes.

Tommy helped his mistress saddle the gold-flecked

Was there anything to do but await the outcome? Yes! If she truly loved Lionel, she could begin to fight for him. If her sister cared not enough for her sibling, and so willingly entered into this fierce competition, it was only fair and fitting that Dorinda return some of the ammunition. She quickly mounted Sunset and led her back to the house. She would need all the time left her that morning to primp and preen herself for the spectacle that was the opening of the Ascot race week.

As Dorinda entered her sister's room, she saw strewn on an overstuffed armchair a flamboyantly feathered hat, the likes of which both she and Edwina had laughed at at the milliner's. Quite obviously, Edwina had returned to the shop and commissioned the article, and was now preparing to sport it. Dorinda wondered how she could let her sister wear such a foolish thing, but then thought to herself how marvelous it would be for Lionel to see her in a hat so thoroughly unbecoming and garish.

Dorie chose for herself a virginal rose-print chiffon dress with a matching sash to tie around her own simple bonnet. She preferred to carry her white gloves in one hand and her closed parasol in the other; these were both part of the expected uniform of the day, all to Dorinda's liking. She stopped at the vanity mirror only to add a discreet blush of rouge to her cheeks; the crisp country air had given her complexion a most natural bloom that demanded no more.

With a regal demeanor, she descended to the patio where she found, as she might have guessed, her sister and Lionel, in the company of George and the marquess.

"You are most ravishing in your ensemble," Lord Ridgely took great pains to tell Dorinda, hoping that his son had noticed as well. "Do you not think so as well, Lionel?"

"Indeed, Father," he answered coolly.

"Mrs. Peg had just brought us a most refreshing lemonade, fortified with just the right amount of gin. May

had chosen to take a fancy to the lady, he thought it was the least he could do to be a perfect guest.

At the racing grounds, the most illustrious of London society was gathered at the royal enclosure, a brilliantly colored canopy pitched on the verdant lawn, to witness the arrival of the Regent and his family, a procession known as the Royal Drive. The Tilburys and the Ridgelys, the Spreaklingers and the twenty-seven other families in line to the throne, all watched as the scarlet-coated outriders led the train of five ornate barouche-landaus, pulled by the finest Windsor grays. The first of the five carriages bore the Regent, bewigged postillions clad in scarlet and gold uniforms riding at his side. At the winning post of the mile-long straightaway, the feast began once the Regent was settled in his garden chair: champagne, caviar, gulls' eggs and Scottish salmon sandwiches, the delicacies befitting a king.

Dorinda could not help noticing that the Regent was in his most comfortable milieu. Surrounded by monied peers and the most beautiful of women attracted by this very regal and festive occasion, he reveled in England's most highly regarded pleasure—the racing of thoroughbreds, all of which could be traced back to the first English Stud Book of 1793, and to those three renowned champions: Byerly Turk, Godolphin Barb, and Darley Arabian, brought to the British Isles at the close of the seventeenth century. The pedigree of all those horses entered in the Ascot races could be traced, on both the side of the sire and the dam, to these. Though Ascot was considered by many to be more spectacle than racing tourney, here could be found the most prized horses in the world.

London's Pride was the finest entry the Tilburys had ever introduced into competition. Her parentage claimed consistent winners in varied racing events, horses such as the legendary Humphrey Clinker, Sorcerer, and Cade.

dered as she watched her father clasp the countess's hand and whisper softly in her ear.

Dorinda thought back to all the times Lionel had shown her such affection and told her how he longed for her, how they belonged together. She remembered his kisses and the gentle caress of his hand against her cheek. How much had been the truth and how much the cruel deceit of a man whose interest wanes as soon as it is returned? She closed her eyes and saw his face in her mind, imagined him kissing her again as she relived the excitement of that special moment they shared in her London drawing room. How artful he was, how believable . . . Or was it that she wanted to believe because she had never met a man as captivating as he? How trusting she had been!

She opened her eyes to find a groom standing in front of her, holding out a glass of champagne in one hand, a platter of tea sandwiches in the other.

"Delightful refreshment," the handsome Viscount Farleigh said as he held up his glass to her.

He had appeared as if from nowhere, and she realized that she had missed the whole of the first race.

"What shall we toast to?" Roderick continued.

"Honesty," Lionel Ridgely answered quickly, as quickly as he stepped between these two.

"Yes, the honesty of men and women alike," Dorinda amended, leaving Roddy to look most curiously from one to the other. Her face had colored at Lionel's boldness, but the blush faded with her response and, after drinking the champagne in one fell swoop, her attention turned away from both men to watch the tourney. Indeed, at that moment it was unthinkable to ponder any situation other than which horse would win the second race!

There was no doubt as to which spectators were most interested by which race, for the rooting was horribly uneven. Those with entries in that day's finale knew

were more of the delicious delicacies for which Ascot was famous—gulls' eggs and Scottish salmon, of course, but also potted beef, poached whiting, fruited breads and tarts, cress and cucumber salads, roasts of venison and mutton.

Dorinda was most delighted by the scene set on the Spanish tiled patio. A natural fence of fir trees, lighted in the encroaching darkness by equidistant torches, formed the boundary for the quadrangle terrace. An orchestra had just begun tuning its instruments when Dorinda first set foot on the tiled terrace. She did not hear the footsteps of the man who followed her outdoors.

"May I claim the first dance?" Lord Farleigh asked her, his blue eyes looking intently at hers, which were sparkling like emeralds.

"Why . . . yes . . . of course," she said, flustered by his sudden appearance. "But I cannot say when the music will begin."

The gallant gentleman took her right hand in his and placed it on his shoulder. "A waltz, please," he requested of the orchestra leader as he took Dorinda's other hand in his.

As if in a dream the music began and he danced her across the floor.

For a time they were the only dancers, though far from being the only ones on the terrace. An audience had formed around this couple who moved like quicksilver through the steps of the waltz.

"With everyone's gaze upon me—" she started to whisper in Roddy's ear, and was about to have him ask the band to stop as summarily as they had begun, but, out of the corner of her eye, she saw Lionel leading Winnie onto the dance floor. She tightened her hold on Roderick's hand and continued to waltz, yet Lionel, unwittingly, held all the thoughts spinning through her head.

Other dancers soon joined the two couples and Dorinda breathed more easily, knowing she could now

"Lionel Ridgely is a dear family friend," she said, "and hardly the one to lay claim to me. I apologize for his interruption, for I much enjoyed your style of dancing," she told him, with a boldness of her own, hoping he would meet the challenge and escort her outside once again.

Indeed, he did.

Dorinda half-expected and had braced herself to see Lionel dancing with her sister. But as they toured the dance floor, she did not see either. It was in fact some time later, when the viscount admitted a thirst for refreshment, that she did learn, once in the parlor, that Lionel had returned to Balmoral House, complaining of a painful migraine, no doubt on the spot of his concussion. He was accompanied home by both his father and Edwina, who had grown tired of dancing with only her papa or "Uncle Ridgely," once Lionel had declared himself unfit for the terrace.

Could she play this game of love? she wondered as she thought of contracting her own migraine as excuse for returning home. Yes, indeed, I must, she said to herself, for I must know what goes on at Balmoral House when only the younger Miss Tilbury is present. In her most endearing voice, she asked the viscount to conduct her home at once.

She bid him good-night on her doorstep, allowing him only the briefest kiss on her hand. She lingered in the foyer fixing her hair in the glass.

"In no uncertain terms," she heard the marchioness state, "I must tell you that your sister has an arrogant fondness for the attentions of numerous gentlemen, rather than those of so sincere a man as my Lionel. And I will not have you voicing any of your silly fears to me simply because, out of sheer politesse, Lionel asked Dorinda for a solitary dance. It is mere courtesy on his part, I can assure you. Under my guidance and direction, you will be

well it could hardly be termed a courtship. "You were aware of Winnie's meddling from the start—and I was not at all intrigued by Lionel, I thought, so I did nothing to stop her. But now, she carries her infatuation too far, especially since I feel Lionel begins to take an interest in me since—Father, are you listening? Father!"

"What is it, dear girl?" he asked in an absent-minded way. He had not heard one word she had said, so distracted was he with the thought of returning to the countess's side. "Can you not discuss your concerns with me on the morrow?" he asked before quitting the room, and without waiting for her reply.

It was obvious to his elder daughter that the earl had been overtaken by a most pervasive emotion, the likes of which she had never seen. Perhaps on the morrow she could make him listen to a word or two, if she could corner him before the start of the second day of races.

for he had watched the horse's progress over the past two years and had been sure she would go on to foal many winning thoroughbreds after her racing life drew to an end. The ankle was bandaged, after being anointed with several liniments to condition the surrounding muscles. The Tilburys left at once for Balmoral House, along with the countess, Dorinda regretfully declining Roderick's invitation to dine at the renowned Savoy Inn.

On the morrow, the Winslows gently exercised London's Pride as the doctor had recommended. The earl and the countess were present, along with Dorinda and George, whose affection for the filly had grown steadily under the enthusiasm of the events. Lionel had stayed home to comfort his stricken mama, and Edwina had contracted another indisposition—the last Dorinda would allow her.

Fight back Dorinda would, and would have stayed at home herself had she not been so concerned with performing her daughterly duties which, presently, entailed being at her father's side to show good spirit even though their prized horse was not in that day's running. She was further saddened by Roddy's absence; his family's business kept him from attending the tourney this afternoon.

It was decided, on the following, final day of the great racing event, that London's Pride should be allowed to run. The veterinarian explained that they were taking a chance, but that the "lady" was not enjoying her confinement. So, she was brought to a trot in the morning, and a gallop in the afternoon, in time for the final competition. London's Pride was the last horse to reach the starting post for the final race that season at Ascot.

The crowd in the royal enclosure was hardly aware of the beginning of the final race, the Ascot Gold Cup. Indeed, Dorinda was animatedly telling both Roderick and Lionel of the elaborate festivities to be held at Balmoral House that evening, to close the race week. She did not

Dorinda could only wish that he had spoken these words to her ears alone, however glad she was that Lionel was at poor George's side. If only he walked to her and took her hands in his, bringing her all his comfort . . . She turned to Roddy.

"It is a sad moment, so fine a horse," Dorinda said.

"But merely a horse, an animal," Roderick said with detachment. There was not even the soft edge of sympathy for Dorinda in his voice. "Your brother will have to learn that a man does not cry at such commonplace occurrences," he added cruelly.

"A horse is nonetheless a living creature, a creation of God. Even a man has the right to weep for something cherished, be it with outward tears or inward suffering," Dorinda said, her eyes wide open to the reasoning of this man who was, outwardly, so sophisticated and worldly, and who now stood before her displaying a hidden insensitivity Dorinda found insufferable. He had broken the spell his charming manner had cast on her, as easily and as quickly. "I am sorry that you will be unable to join us at Balmoral House this evening. I am certain Ascot will not be quite the same without you," she added, in these few words communicating to him the fact that she never wished to see him again.

How could she have let herself be taken in a second time? she wondered. But as she watched Lionel with George, she thought that perhaps the first case had not been a deception after all. Perhaps it had just taken her longer to see that the kindness in Lionel's nature was the stronger of the two conflicting forces in his personality, the other being his self-assurance. Even that, Dorinda mused, was beguiling.

"Father, I think it best to take George home," she told the earl.

"Certainly. I will attend to the details and follow you," he replied, tenderly caressing the countess's hand.

Safe within the pink phaeton, George buried his head

could the more desperate realities of life. She hitched Sunset to the familiar tree and began walking toward the brook. She thought she heard a noise in the distance, and a smile came to her lips when she saw Lionel in the distance. Her expression soon changed to one of ennui when she heard Edwina's prattling voice. She moved closer to listen, knowing she shouldn't—but her curiosity took control of her better nature.

"I love the country . . . it is so romantic, the perfect place for lovers," Winnie said shockingly, as she toyed with her hair.

"The beauty of the country is undeniable, but I love the sea," Lionel told her. "There is nothing quite like the marvelous perfection of its creation, the tranquility of the shore, the soft grains of sand. Yes, Chichester is the most peaceful spot in all the world; my grandmother's limestone house is there on the shore, home for me while my parents traveled across the Continent. There I feel a sense of freedom; there are no cares when you walk along the beach and gaze at the water reaching so far into the distance that you can never see its limits. It is a place for thought and reflection, where you can be free," he told her, confessing an aspect of his nature that Dorinda had never seen.

"I love the sea as well," Edwina was quick to add. "The seashore is a wonderful haven for lovers, too."

"It has been far too long since I visited there," he reflected. "My business enterprises in London keep me from the pleasures I most enjoy."

"London is too hectic a place for lovers," Edwina answered. "It is impossible to savor the romance of courtship when there are so many duties to be attended to." She spoke far more boldly than Dorinda had ever heard.

"I think it's time we returned to the house," Lionel said, feeling a sense of uneasiness at being alone with her.

"Must we?" she asked as he rose.

"No more than you enjoyed the attentions of the Viscount Farleigh—Lord Roddy, was it not?" he retorted hotly.

"You witnessed the end of that ill-fated friendship. I have renounced his advances, and yet you compare my actions to your consummate flirtation with my sister!"

"And what of Felix-and-Arthur? Certainly it was not friendship on their collective mind when I walked into that charming patio scene last week," he retorted. His anger won out over his better sense, which told him Dorinda could never truly love either of the dandies.

"Surely you cannot equate your penchant for my sister with their fraternal interest in me! Surely you cannot object to my having friends other than yourself, when you choose to be away from my side more often than not!" she said, far exceeding her own limits of propriety.

"Perhaps it is that I do not wish my name to be linked so casually with theirs, even by the noble bond of friendship," he said, his dark eyes blazing ominously.

"I believe you toy with my sister and myself far too much, and are perhaps pitting one against the other, Lionel Ridgely. For you cannot make the same heartfelt demands on both of us—I'll not allow it! Today you wish me to consider you apart from all others, and yet until now, you did not even wish to speak to me, much less have me hold you in such high esteem," she said, explaining her doubts of his sincerity.

"That was my anger manifesting itself, not my heart, Dorie," he said in a much gentler voice.

"Your anger? What had provoked it?"

"An ungracious welcome into this house," he began. "I cannot conceal my feelings and thoughts—it concerns one conversation whose exchange reached my ears: your discussion with your father on the night of our arrival. It was after I retired . . . I was sorry to hear that I had miserably misinterpreted your affection for me."

12

"Dorinda Tilbury is completely unsuitable as the wife of my son!"

It would have been impossible for any woman entering the foyer of her own home not to linger ever so innocently in that foyer to listen for the explanation to follow. So Dorie casually stared at her reflection in the glazed foyer mirror while the marchioness told why she found Miss Tisbury inadequate.

"It is obvious to me that Dorinda is no longer the sweet young thing she was at her come-out, for now she dangles her suitors like monkeys on a string, and I will not have Lionel counted among them. She has lost that Dorinda was not meant to hear, but to which the young sister," the marchioness continued, speaking words Dorinda was not meant to hear, but to which the young girl listened nonetheless. "In all actuality, I do not see where Lionel must be coerced into marriage—it certainly did not improve your disposition," she commented wryly.

Here the marquess could not contain his patience. "The state of marriage has little to do with the discontent of our situation. You cannot be ignorant of the fact that we have not had a marriage in any but the legal sense for a number of years—"

"What has this to do with Lionel?" she interrupted, hoping to keep him from pursuing that vein.

143

former track of their conversation. "I would suggest Edwina."

"And why not Dorinda? She is the oldest and has known Lionel for many a year—it is most natural. I find her sister too coquettish," Lord Ridgely stated.

"Not at all! I have talked to the girl at great length and she is a charm, a marvel," his wife insisted. "She is refreshingly admirable and her love for Lionel is quite genuine."

"How can you know this is not simply a child's infatuation, as I have interpreted it these past weeks?" he said, maintaining his side of the debate.

"That is a possibility, Carlton. But you have not questioned the girl as I have," she retorted, with a smug smile.

"At what length?" he asked, unwilling to drop the challenge. "I fear you have encouraged her, not merely questioned . . ."

"I have discreetly inquired and I am sure of one thing. She has no jaded past that can be rubbed in my son's face at a future date!" Fiona Ridgely was convinced.

"A jaded past? Dorinda Tilbury? How can you say such a thing after all the pains her father has taken to make her the worthiest prize in all of London. It is Dorinda and not Edwina—"

"Father, say no more!" Lionel demanded, as he strode through the wood-framed doors that led from the patio. "I'm certain you have got both ladies' ears burning," he said, not knowing how true that was, for Dorinda at least. "And I'll have no more of it. You'll not speak of our hostesses in such a manner again, not when I do indeed mean to make one of them my wife!"

"But which one?" the marchioness gasped, refusing to relent.

"You will know all in good time. But for the present, that is all. I will not have you intrude on what will be a

ed. "Because I have found myself a beau, the one you chose to discard?"

"When did I toss Lionel aside? When did I ever give you cause to believe that I stopped caring for him?"

"The night you arrived in Ascot and told father you would not marry him—*before* the man had come up to scratch! I can't believe you do not remember. Your voice was loud enough for all in the house to hear, Lionel included," Winnie freshened her memory.

Dorinda was dumbstruck. So that was the conversation Lionel had alluded to earlier, she thought, feeling a great emptiness in the center of her stomach.

"Dorinda, you have forsaken all chance you had with Lionel and it is my turn, one which I fully intend to take, for truly I love him. It is not an infatuation, as you might wish to believe. I feel my heart pound when I am with him, speaking openly about how we feel, not wasting time with meaningless pleasantries like the weather or the latest cricket match. And you cannot open and close the doors of your heart like the doors of a house, and you can *certainly* not persuade me to do the same," she argued boldly. "I will not stop pursuing Lionel, not even for you, my sister. And if you choose to break with me, then so be it."

On that unpleasant note, Edwina sauntered from the room, the garish hat of purple-colored plumes precariously perched on the very top of her head.

Where had her sister found such cruel words? Dorinda wondered. She bemoaned the kind of woman Winnie seemed destined to become: selfish, arrogant, and heartless. How could Dorinda help her? Surely there must be a way—she had most certainly lost Lionel; she could not bear to lose the love of her young sister.

Was there no end to the heartaches love caused? Even after the difficulties of a courtship, would she find herself in the unhappy predicament of the marquess and his wife?

for the pleasure of riding them, that they needn't be raced to be enjoyed. We can take an interest in their swiftness, their agility, the continuation of the line of a particular breed. There is no reason to want to continually prove a horse's superiority by racing it," the countess opined, challenging the primary reason the Tilbury family came to Ascot. Yet Edmund Tilbury was so taken with this beautiful woman, there was no doubting that she could entreat him to adopt her point of view. For Dorinda's part, if it meant no longer risking the lives of the other horses, and that of the new foal in particular, she agreed wholeheartedly.

"It seems time to change our usual routine," the earl claimed, embracing Alicia's opinion, and her hand as well. "And we shall have the bash as usual tomorrow evening, this time to celebrate the end of our days at the races. I was of a mind to cancel the party, but now I am in better humor. It will be a celebration of varied kinds," he added, leading his daughter to wonder if there wasn't something he, and the countess, had neglected to tell her.

"Delightful," Alicia told him. "I shall assist with whatever preparations are necessary."

"I think it best to confer with Cook and Mrs. Garetty. They are no doubt awaiting my instructions," the earl said, and took his leave to meet with the staff.

"Won't you sit down?" the countess said, patting the seat beside her.

"I would like to speak with you . . . if that is all right. The topic of conversation I have in mind might seem presumptuous," she said timidly, but the countess's endearing expression gave her encouragement. "I have no woman friend, other than my sister, with whom I can share my innermost feelings. . . . It is at a time such as this that I miss my mother, her understanding, and her compassion. You have become nearly one of the family in such a short time that I thought perhaps this not too intimate to broach with you."

can tell when his interest is aroused," the countess told her with all honesty.

"But I fear he compares me to my sister and, if the truth be known, that he has taken a fancy to her over me," she confessed, feeling some relief in saying her fears aloud.

"You cannot abandon your love so easily," Alicia warned. "You have no reason to lose heart or feel vanquished. Although I have come to know you more intimately than your sister—for she does take greater pains to be at Lionel's side than to converse with any of her other guests—it is not out of partiality that I say I am convinced that Lionel's greatest feelings of affection are for you, and not Edwina. Lionel is a smart young man; he cannot be unaware of the fact that Winnie is in her first breath of womanhood and cannot know her own mind, nor fathom the complexities of a man such as Lionel.

"I am not saying it will be an assured victory. Apart from Edwina, there are many other women who would seek his attentions. But you are the only one to have him in your own home. It would be foolhardy not to take full advantage of the fact. With the races at an end, there is no knowing when he may decide to quit the country. You must act at once and in a forthright way, though not half as obviously as your sister," the countess suggested.

"But how do I approach him? What are the appropriate things to say?" Dorinda asked, eager for the knowledge of the countess's experienced years. "I am not at all well versed in the art of seduction."

"If you are enamored of one another, it is not a seduction," the countess quickly pointed out. "It is more like an argument—but you must persuade Lionel that you are both in agreement. In subtle ways, you must show him how you feel about him. You might ask that he be your escort at tomorrow's bash, as even a lady in her own home will benefit from the presence of a man at her side."

The sky was ablaze with colors of deep red and blue and violet. The fiery orange sun loomed so large that Dorinda thought they might touch it, and then, perhaps, not have to remember the sadder moments of life.

"We cannot let ourselves be tainted by the arguments we are each so adept at creating," Dorinda declared. "We must sign a truce."

"Yes," he agreed, and would have sealed his concurrence with a kiss had she been turned to face him.

"I must also thank you for your kind attention to George. You accorded him the respect of a man when he felt he was acting too much the little boy," Dorinda said, voicing George's fears.

"I was there to comfort you as well, but thought you would have none of it," Lionel admitted frankly.

"And I thought your presence was for George's sake alone," she confessed. "How, without spoken words, can we prevent such confusion?"

"Do you not remember my toast to honesty?" he asked. "It shall be our watchword."

"Will you now tell me why you quit London? Was it to visit your mama?" she asked with all the courage in her soul. She had tried to bury the question, but it often sprang forward in her mind. She waited expectantly for his reply.

"I was in Worcester, hoping to smooth the differences in my cousin Maxine's marriage. Had I not told you? I was certain that I mentioned it in Dorking. But alas, I was no more successful there than with my own parents this afternoon.

"I am certain now that it takes more than love for a marriage to last, but it stands not a chance without it. I believe that Maxine and her husband love each other, and yet they cannot repair grave differences in their characters that gnaw away at their love. My parents do not have that love to begin with, and because of that they do not even attempt to reconcile those differences which wrench them

153

too hot for freshly cooked puddings, yet the fruits for open tarts were already stewing. Four large legs of lamb were skewered and prepared for cooking over the open fire just beyond the kitchen doors.

Two gardeners were cutting roses from the bushes and collecting the more beautiful of the wildflowers that, if the truth be told, were quite artfully growing along the arrangement Lady Tilbury had once prescribed. Dorinda searched the kitchen shelves for all the crystal finery needed, particularly the tall vases that would be filled and arranged throughout the house to create an exotic effect.

Butler assisted Bucky and young Bobby Winslow in the sweeping and airing of rooms. All the window latches had been opened and the house filled with a fresh country breeze that cooled the hot edges of the summer morning.

Winnie, though furious at her sister's bold actions of the former day, which led her, the night before, to accuse Dorie of stealing her beau, still followed Dorinda's instruction to spruce and plump the decorative pillows in the commons room, all carefully embroidered by Eloise over the course of her brief lifetime.

The house was a beehive of activity with even the earl pitching in to move aside one of the heavier sofa tables so the room might accomodate more of the friends and neighbors who yearly graced his house on this day.

Toward the early afternoon, Dorinda was mixing large pitchers of mead, the honeyed wine favored by Englishmen since the time of Queen Elizabeth. There was always one drink or dish that could be termed "old-fashioned," to remind everyone of England's great past and summon images of an even greater future. There would also be great goblets of lemonade and ale, to be circulated by Butler, as soon as the guests started to arrive, a few hours later, *at twilight,* as the invitations read.

The countess, in diaphanous periwinkle silk gown, was at the earl's side to greet their friends. Lord Went-

13

Dorinda climbed the stairs and walked toward her father's library, the only possible place for Lionel's retreat. As she approached, she heard two voices and recognized them both.

It was with an engulfing feeling of horror that she listened to the following exchange.

"Though we have only known each other a short time, I find the thought of not living each waking moment at your side unbearable. You are in my thoughts at every opportunity, in my mind, my heart, my every breath, always. I love you. Will you be my wife?" Lionel asked.

At this timely interval, Dorinda peered, unnoticed, into the room. She had to see to truly believe that her ears did not deceive her. The sight only added to her mortification.

Lionel was poised on one knee and held Edwina's hand. They sat by the window, the perfect scene for a tapestry, Dorinda thought regretfully.

"Yes, yes, I accept!" she answered with glee. "I cannot think of anything that could give me more happiness."

Dorinda braced herself against the wall and stood with amazement as she witnessed her sister's joy. She slowly retraced her steps down the corridor, returning to their chamber before rejoining her guests below. She was

thought me the 'lovesick puppy' clinging to you so desperately. And to think of the heartache I have caused Dorinda . . . she loves you, Lionel, I am certain of it. She was not aware of it at first. She tried terribly to hate you, but could not. It is only that her pride, not her true heart, that often voices its own false opinion. And if she should put you down a peg when you come up to scratch, I'll box her ears!" she said, telling him she was his ally. "My other hope is that my sister will forgive my part in this. What could I have been thinking to put aside my sisterly feelings and think her my foe? She must think me the most wretched sibling on earth. Perhaps you will explain to her all you have told me, so that she might understand and forgive my . . . infatuation, as you so delicately termed it."

"Dorinda is a wise woman," Lionel said proudly. "I am convinced she has known of your puppy heart these past weeks and has been more amused than angry that her little sister was becoming a young lady." He hoped to lessen her concern.

"I am afraid that you did not hear the torrent of anger let loose in the chamber we are presently forced to share. I defended my feelings to the end, I'm afraid, told her that I would fight both parent and sibling for you," Winnie admitted, as she grew a brilliant red. "Not a genteel sight, I might add."

"Perhaps her heart would more readily soften if you were to tell her I wish to see her here and now. You could be dubbed Eros just for tonight," he said teasingly.

"I will do anything you wish to make amends for my intolerable behavior," she said, still ashamed of her naiveté. Her father, her sister, Peg—all had tried to warn her that her emotions were far too advanced for her age, but she had had to hear the words from Lionel's own lips. And how thoughtfully and patiently he had told of his everlasting love for her sister—which began the very day

was camouflaged by the strong support of the countess, well used to her late husband's fainting spells, another souvenir of his voyages to India.

The marquess of Beaumont made his way to the earl's side, a most inquisitive expression on his face.

"Edmund, can this be a lark?" he asked in whispers.

The marchioness, at her husband's side for the first time that night, ignored these comments and gave Edmund a kiss upon his cheek. "Hearty felicitations on this blessed day," she offered. "I am certain your daughter and her fiancé will be most happy together. From what I have seen this past week, they get on quite ideally."

The earl had never, in all these years, fancied having one thing in common with the baron (or was it Mr. Horatio—he very much considered them interchangeable). But now they did share the same paralyzing surprise, which had the effect of turning them to stone figures.

Dorinda found that her words had a strange effect on her own self as well. She knew not what to say to all her guests, friends, neighbors, acquaintances who flocked 'round her, pressing her for the romantic details. They congratulated her for something she had done out of hurt pride, not love. The air of gaiety was utterly false. She had not thought before acting, had merely followed through on the first notion that had entered her mind. Now here she was, ready to burst a dam once more at the thought of losing Lionel, and to her sister, whom she so dearly loved. Yes, she had lost Winnie as well. But the cruelest part of this abysmal affair was that Dorinda realized her own arrogance and coldness had propelled Lionel into the hands of her sister. She recounted in her mind the many times, since the beginning of their reacquaintance, that Winnie had been at his side. It was not simply these days in Ascot, but had been the ritual since the first time he called on her at home. While Dorie had been in town, Winnie would entertain him at the Tilbury

"What have I done? I must insist you account for your own actions before you ask for an explanation of mine," she answered, reminding Winnie of her seniority.

"That was precisely what I was going to offer as I asked for a moment's attention, but that plan was drawn before the scene I have just witnessed unfolded. How can you commit yourself to a man who does not hold your interest?" Winnie asked.

"And where did you cultivate such an impression?" Dorie countered.

"It has been obvious to me for more than the past two months that Lionel Ridgely is the only man who holds your fancy," Winnie explained.

"Is that why you chose to pursue him and let him divide two sisters?"

"I made a dreadful mistake, Dorie. He has made me realize that my feelings were premature—it was not love," Winnie began.

"I think you have consumed far too much champagne, Edwina, because you do not make any sense. It was not a half hour ago that I heard you accept a most enticing proposal of marriage from Mr. Ridgely," Dorie told her.

"Oh, good heavens! The plan is scotched!" Winnie exclaimed, covering her face with her hands.

"Yes, indeed—were you hoping to keep it a secret?" Dorinda asked, her broken heart taking the form of a heated temper.

"Dorinda, you have worsened the mess I made of things. You overheard Lionel's brilliant proposal, but did not stay to hear the conclusion and, obviously, had not arrived in time to hear his opening comments," her sister continued.

"The precious parts I heard were sufficient," Dorie stated plainly.

"I think not, for the words of love were not meant for me, but were merely a rehearsal destined in its final

Lionel, at a few feet's distance, conversing with one Count Tybor. The expression on Mr. Ridgely's face told the ladies that they had lost all chance of postponing the distressing news.

Dorinda, impossibly furious with herself, could not bear to share the company of even those guests she cherished enough to call friends. She quickly left the room to sequester herself in her bedchamber where she would, until coaxed out, remain.

Winnie could not escape the scene as easily. Lionel approached and seized her arm tightly. He did not speak at first, his eyes flashing the question on his mind.

"It is a mistake," Winnie said with great difficulty. It was as though his iron grip prevented her from breathing, speaking, thinking.

"Yes, indeed, a mistake that I chose to love her. I should have realized at the start what a devious coxcomb she was," he said before his anger gave way to sadness.

"No, Lionel. You do not understand—" she tried to explain as she wrestled for possession of her arm. "Dorinda misunderstood—she was—"

"Do not offer your feeble explanations. I have heard enough from such unkind lips to last an eternity, you little conspiratrice. I have met many women such as you, women who prey upon a sincere man. It was my own foolhardiness that prompted me to think, after meeting so many London wenches, that I had found one with a tender heart. And that I let you both take me in. To be so cruelly deceived!" he said and thrust Winnie's hand away.

"Lionel, Lionel, please listen, for but a moment," she said, clasping her hands on his shoulders to gain his attention.

His eyes darted about the room, he seethed with the anger and despair of a caged cat waiting for his chance to seize his freedom. "There can be no explanation for your treachery, Miss Tilbury. Oh, had I but listened to my mother, who tried to warn me against the charms of a

broad grin. He held an anticipation of his own—when not causing family calamities, he delighted in watching others carry them out.

The earl was about to launch a discourse on the ladies' behavior when the marquess and his wife entered the room, battling all the while. They were followed by the countess, who sat down at the earl's left and gently held his hand, which seemed to lessen his fury somewhat. Tempers hovered at great heights and it seemed fortunate indeed that the good Dr. Warren Wheatly was still in attendance, in the event that one of these people should be subject to a seizure.

"I will tell you all," the marchioness began, "I am well satisfied with the turn events have taken, for I do not believe Miss Dorinda to be the proper match for my darling Lionel, however charming she portends to be."

The marquess rose from his chair and leaned over the table toward his wife and exclaimed, "I order you to leave this house at once! I'll not tolerate such rude behavior toward our hosts!"

"And I will not have you speak that way of my sister!" Edwina told the marchioness, rising to her feet, and to her sister's defense.

"And I will speak for myself, for as the senior Miss Tilbury, I must set the example of communicating my true feelings, no longer at the mercy of the dwarfing manners of the *ton,* the true instigators in this sorrowful incident," Dorinda stated eloquently.

"A lady of your tender years will not raise your voice to me," the marchioness countered before her husband clapped his hand over her mouth.

Lord Tilbury's voice was the next to be raised in anger. "Carlton, perhaps it will be best for you and me to resolve this matter in my library. And Lionel should be present as well, so that we might discuss this as men. It is obvious the women cannot keep their heads!"

"But where is Lionel?" George asked, certain that

14

Edmund Tilbury turned to his eldest daughter. Her face was now buried in the cup of her hands.

"I hope you have an explanation for the grave incident which has transpired under my nose, but which only now fully arouses my sensibilities," he said, his blue eyes as cold as frost on a windowpane.

While Peg passed platters of corned beef hash and new potatoes, peach porridge and fresh sausage, Dorinda, aided by Winnie, recounted the most recent misunderstanding between Lionel and herself.

"So you see, Father, I was convinced that his proposal was for Winnie. Out of my own hurt pride, I turned to devoted Arthur."

"And Lionel refused to listen to my explanation, that Dorinda had misunderstood after overhearing our conversation," Winnie added. "He was as perverse as she, his belief being that Dorie loved the baron and had chosen him over Lionel."

Edmund sighed heavily and, for once, the distress was not assuaged in any way by the tender consolations of the lovely countess.

"Could you not at least have chosen his titled brother for your folly?" the earl asked.

" 'Twas Felix's cousin, not Arthur's brother, dear

ment to my dear friend," the baron said, hoping to save his neck—somehow—from both the block and the church.

"It will be impossible for you to remain in Ascot, I'm sure of it—you are well aware of the gossipmongers of the region. We must take great pains to contrive a story that is tightly knit and fully cohesive, for it would hold grave consequences were we found out," the earl insisted.

"I will quit England if that is the solution," Hapsley said boldly. "Felix has already consented to be my companion, and we are not for want of funds. It has been far too long since I have promised myself the Grand Tour abroad, and though I am of more advanced age than most of the young brats of wealthy parentage, it is not unbecoming a journey."

"Indeed, but we can not have it going about that you have taken it in your head to suddenly renounce my daughter's fancy and sail across the sea. We are wanting of a legitimate and reasonable explanation," Edmund warned, worried after his daughter's reputation.

"Perhaps Arthur can be abducted!" Mr. Horatio proffered. "I can don a disguise and hold you for a king's ransom."

"I do not find that at all sufficient," Lord Tilbury said, trying to hide his disgust. "For then it falls on our shoulders to reclaim the baron—and I'll not have his death on my conscience!"

"Would you then kill me?" Arthur asked his friend, shocked at the earl's implications.

"To prevent discovery I must! But that won't do at all," Felix admitted, and replaced his thinking bonnet.

"Certainly not!" Arthur echoed.

"But what if a relation abducted you—not abducted, of course," Dorinda began, "but summoned you? On a matter of extreme urgency? Family necessity takes you from my side, and I, kind and tender-hearted, agree to wait a reasonable length of time for your return. I will

"Think not upon it," Arthur said, taking her left hand.

"No, not at all," Felix added, seizing the right. "For we had planned such a tour for the fall. It is only that we travel sooner."

"We will correspond and you will let us know of your Mr. Ridgely," Arthur said.

"Yes, Mr. Ridgely," Felix echoed. "We know all about him! His presence here disappointed poor Roddy ... yes, indeed."

"I am sorry if I disappointed *you* by not sharing this precious confidence. But I have never loved before and it is all so exciting and distressing, so infuriating and so wonderfully satisfying all at the same time.

"You begin your journey as I begin mine. Mr. Ridgely has disappeared and I must find him before his broken heart leads him to as disastrous a decision as I reached yesterday," she said, and then watched them withdraw.

Alone in the garden, Dorinda began to formulate her own plan, but she did not know where it would take her. Would Lionel have returned to London? Or perhaps to Tunbridge Wells? Which?

She sat upon the grass under the great sycamore tree and looked toward the sky, wondering if she and Lionel shared the same view. She thought back upon their brief yet turbulent courtship, thought of all the moments they had spent together, hoping she would find a hint as to where he had taken himself. Then she remembered his words ...

The beauty of the country is undeniable, but I love the sea ... the tranquility of the shore, the soft grains of the sand. Yes, Chichester is the most peaceful spot in all the world. My grandmother's limestone house ... freedom ... a place for thought ... without a care ...

Dorinda rose to her feet and ran as speedily as they would carry her to the carriage house. She found Bucky

173

"Lionel has told you about me?" Dorinda asked, gleeful that she was still in his thoughts.

"I hope you are here to offer him an explanation. He is a man who has let his feelings be known for the first time, only to find himself strung up by them," Lady Simpson said, waiving the usual formalities.

"I love your grandson," Dorinda said with a heavy heart. "I am here to tell him so."

"Then you had best do it at once. You'll find him with eager ears. What time is it?" she then asked, leaving Dorinda to wonder what bearing that information would have on their conversation.

"Just past eleven," a maid answered dutifully.

"Then you will find Lionel walking on the beach with Oscar," Lady Simpson said, pointing the way.

"Oscar?" Dorinda asked with piqued curiosity.

"His Labrador, of course."

At the top of the stone stairs that led to the beach, Dorinda could see Lionel's robust figure running along the shoreline with Oscar nipping at his heels. He and Oscar were chasing after a large, bright colored rubber ball, but the dog lost interest when he saw the young lady appear, and his barking told his master of her presence. Oscar ran toward her in leaps and bounds, his wet coat casting a shower of seadrops on the fine gold sand. Lionel looked only briefly into those fiery emerald eyes and turned away.

Dorinda, improperly dressed in rose taffeta, lifted her skirts and followed him away from the manor. But her delicately heeled shoes sank into the mud and inhibited her pursuit, so enraging her that she cast them into the sea. With bared feet, she ran after him, pleading with him all the way to ease his pace so that she might catch her breath.

"Lionel!" Dorinda screamed out as he walked far-

was a mistake. If we had been free to admit our feelings to each other, if we had been able to enjoy their blossoming without the pressure of our parents, perhaps none of this turmoil would have come about, perhaps you and I would not find ourselves on this shore, so far removed from the life we know," she said, before thinking of how particularly pleasing it was to find herself alone with Lionel, far from both families. "Lionel, I will say it now one thousand times if it will convince you to forgive me. I love you."

"Dorinda," he said softly, pressing her against his breast. "I doubt I can tell you how much I love you. A man is neither to be overtaken by emotion, by love or by jealousy, and yet both those passions have found a home in my heart, from the day we first met. When I saw you with Hapsley, my good senses should have prevailed, but did not. I stubbornly chose to see something greater than friendship between you, and played upon your sister to irk you. My jealousy found it not at all implausible that you would choose to marry him, though by that evening I had thought it exorcized. Perhaps a stronger man would have walked over to you and congratulated you on your news, as did your other guests. But I could not stand and watch your hands clasped in his while you were toasted. I could not suffer the loss of you," he confessed openly.

"No, Lionel, not a stronger man, but only one with less tenderness could have witnessed the scene you did and been able to hide his discomfiture. It is because you are the kind of man who is aware of passion that I love you. It was that very love which blinded me to my sister's infatuation. I should have realized that you would return her affection with kindness, but my reason was tinged with envy that led me to think you bestowed love, not friendship, on Winnie.

"If only we could have told each other of our love, our feelings and our fears . . ." Dorinda mused with regret.

177

15

The bride wore a gray-blue silk gown, with a modest lace veil covering her eyes. The groom looked dashing in his black afternoon attire, complete with top hat and cane. They were married at the small Ascot chapel, by the Reverend Jones James, the Tilbury clergyman since Dorinda could remember. The short ceremony bound the woman to the man, for better and for worse.

There was a small reception in the parish garden, made festive with champagne and petit fours, the pastry of French kings. Dorinda kissed the bridal couple, and she and her sister sent the new Lady Tilbury and her husband, Lord Edmund, on a honeymoon jaunt to Paris. It was left to George who, in his top hat and tails, was his father's best man, to throw a spray of rice high into the air, to shower the newlyweds with prayers for happiness. It was a joyous occasion, for all save the Ridgelys, who, husband and wife, each bemoaned the loss of a friend to a spouse. At the Ascot manor unfolded a scene of chaos orchestrated by the marchioness, as she gathered her belongings, with the help of Mrs. Garetty. It was left to Peg to frequently retrieve from the guest's portmanteau Tilbury possessions such as an ormolu pillbox or a lavender sachet pillow (to name but two examples) which—somehow—found their way into the suitcase.

Despite her propensity for coveting objects not her

what it was they each longed for the most, their dreams for the future. They conversed on the topics of young lovers: the excitement of traveling to exotic lands, the home they planned to build, the children they hoped to conceive, the happiness they felt at sharing all together. They vowed not to grow into meddlesome parents, as both their fathers had, but realized it would be impossible not to want to guide one's offspring toward what was thought the proper direction.

Lionel held Dorinda's hand so that they might both look into the glistening diamond of the ring on Dorinda's third finger. Grandmother Simpson had given it to her future daughter-in-law before she and Lionel quit Chichester. A symbol of their love, she had called it, a promise for the future. It shone like the brightest star in the heavens, and Dorinda saw reflected in its many facets all her hopes and prayers for their life together.

Lionel's attentiveness kept her from feeling the sadness of quitting the house in Ascot. She had closed the door that had led to many happy times, as a child and as a young woman. Apart from London, Ascot was the only home she had ever known, but, with Lionel at her side, she realized that there was an entire world left to be explored and conquered. Soon their memories would be of times spent together, of shared joy.

As they passed the town of Dorking, Lionel squeezed her hand, reminding them both of the tenderness she had shown him.

"I daresay that episode will make an interesting tale for our grandchildren," he said, but then, seeing her blush, changed his mind. "Perhaps we shall keep the secret of that time to ourselves, for I doubt any could appreciate it as greatly as I." He gave the reins of the phaeton to his beloved, keeping his arms around her all the while she expertly conducted the carriage. Together, the journey passed all too quickly, or so it seemed to the lovers.

That opinion was not shared by the riders in the

bedclothes, certainly some china and crystal. And a million and one other things to be discovered in a shop's window."

Silver, lace, crystal—Winnie had been correct. These formed the main part of their purchases and Bucky, who followed them in the pink phaeton, was quite well exercised by the end of the day, as he had to jump from the box at frequent intervals to gather their parcels and place them within the coach. But there was one purchase that did not occur to either of the young ladies until later that night.

"I am in a most perplexing quandary," Dorinda began. "I have furnishings, a bridal gown, the mainstay of my trousseau—but no home to put them all in. I must begin a search for a house in London."

Dorinda waited until the next visit from Lionel to discuss this imminent matter with him. He decided that it was all too necessary indeed to consult someone entirely knowledgeable in the field.

The next week was an utter delight to Dorinda for, at the side of her fiancé, she embarked on her house-shopping expedition, and discovered what she thought were among the most exclusive townhouses in London. Lionel's yearly income, combined with the dowry she would bring to the marriage, would more than suffice for the maintenance of the perfect abode—if only she could choose from among the rare jewels she had been shown in such fashionable neighborhoods as Russell Square, St. James Place and Bromley Street.

There were houses with thatched roofs, limestone mansions, and red-brick edifices with a certain worldly charm. What was preferable? she had to ask herself: four bedchambers-three fireplaces-two sitting rooms, or three bedchambers-five fireplaces-one sitting room and a library, or eight bedchambers-ten fireplaces and one garret? What could she use as a guide? Her own home had an equal number of each!

held the hand to her chest and asked, "Sister, can you feel my heart pounding?"

"'Tis perfectly natural," Winnie assured her, "for you are marrying your very own Prince Charming, as the fairy stories say. The thought of being married to Lionel Ridgely would put the goose upon my flesh as well!"

"And how can you be so sure that he is my prince?" Dorinda asked.

"I have read it in all the novellas, of course," Winnie stated matter-of-factly.

"What novellas?"

"Those of Miss Austen, for one," Winnie confessed. "I have been . . . perusing the lady's books . . . in private . . ."

"And Miss Austen explains the pounding as normal?" Dorie asked, willing to put credence in the experience of the author who, she did not know, had never married.

"Yes, of course. Why do you doubt it?" Winnie asked.

"It is only because—" and here she paused, hoping to phrase her doubt in words that Winnie would understand without hesitation. "It is that I have spent these past few years decidedly not falling in love. And then, all of a sudden, I meet a strangely wonderful man and am willing to dedicate my life to his happiness. Has it happened all too soon? What will prevent me from letting another man capture my fancy as easily? It is so perplexing."

But Edwina was ready with a reply.

"Your lack of interest in any other young eligible easily explains that you have been patiently waiting for the right man to wander along. If Lionel Ridgely piques you in a way that no other does, then it is even more obvious that he is your man! I am sure of your love for him, even if you are not, for I have carefully watched it

their purchases for the approving eyes of both *père et mère,* Dorinda noticeably more entranced by the proceedings than her sister. It was only when the former countess produced a special bundle of parcels for Edwina and George did their eyes alight.

"This lilac silk will make the perfect fabric for a come-out gown, don't you agree?" Alicia Tilbury asked her younger step-daughter. "And this sailboat will create the greatest to-do at the Regent's Pond in Green Park," she said to George.

The little family still had many more parcels to undo, and the ladies forged ahead. The earl was so pleased at the scene unfolding before him that he did not notice the short lived look of happiness in his son's eyes. It did not return when he was presented with a dozen *livres de poche,* nor the Frenchman's beret, though his donning of the hat caused quite a riotous scene.

"Is this the way to wear it?" George asked impatiently, as the hat sunk low over his forehead.

"It is to be worn up high, and tilted to one side," his father explained, but not quickly enough. Before he could help the boy adjust the beret, George cast it aside and quit the room.

"Too much excitement," Dorie said, hoping to smooth over the incident. "A full night's sleep will mend his quick temper. I'm afraid we have been a bit over-indulgent in your absence . . . he will come 'round on the morrow."

But the tranquil atmosphere that had pervaded was now lost and showed no sign of returning the following day, at least wherein George was concerned. The earl left his wife to assume the management of the family and George, well used to the tolerant hand of his beloved Peg Garetty and the lenient attitude of his sisters, was not familiar was the strictness of a concerned mother.

He balked at great length when it was suggested by Alicia Tilbury that he might begin to learn French, rather

growing more imminent by the day, it came as no surprise that George's confusion took the form of angry tantrums at near every possible opportunity. When the summer came to its close, and the wedding fully upon them, George's anger turned to apprehension and fear, and took a most terrifying manifestation the very night before the ceremony. It was after one of his frequent battles with his new mama—on the perennial subject of French lessons—that George, perhaps in cahoots with Master Leroy, packed a small satchel, slung it haphazardly over one shoulder, and quit the house.

As the elder Tilburys were celebrating at the bridal soirée given by Lady Aster, Lionel's paternal aunt, they were unaware of the boy's departure until they returned to Park Lane to find Peg frantically tearing her hair. She had searched the house twice when the boy did not appear for his supper, but couldn't locate him. Lord Tilbury would have summoned Scotland Yard had not a servant appeared at the front door, bearing a note from Master Leroy's parents, explaining that the two boys had sequestered themselves in a nearby treehouse, right under the nose of a neighborhood busybody who did not delay in reporting the scene to the proper authority. The earl was shocked and greatly angered that his son would cause new havoc in their lives, and was of no fit mind to collect the boy from his hideaway. Fortunately for George's neck, his elder sister volunteered to lead the recovery expedition, with Lionel at her side in the pink phaeton.

They rode 'round to the park opposite Marlborough Place where the treehouse could be found.

"Can you climb a tree, my love?" Lionel asked as he drew the horses to a halt.

"I have climbed more than a hundred, Lionel Ridgely," she responded confidently and tied up her skirts in a manner she knew well.

When she reached the landing on which the small

ours and the Ridgelys. But you must make me the promise of giving your trust and love to our new mother. Remember that we have each other, but Alicia is alone in our house, with no one but us to call family. Father is a wise man, for he found in his new wife all the qualities he has long missed in his first, our mother.

"I know that it is a great deal for you to accept all at once, but if we make the effort together, you will soon see that I am right. Have we struck a bargain?" Dorinda asked, and laughed inwardly, thinking of how alike she and her father were after all. George nodded his assent.

She looked out from the treehouse toward Lionel standing below, an expression of adoration in his eyes. She realized that she had indeed fulfilled her promise to her father. And tomorrow, she thought to herself, the pink phaeton would be rightfully hers.